USA TODAY bestselling and RITA® Award–
nominated author **Caitlin Crews** loves writing
romance. She teaches her favourite romance novels
in creative writing classes at places like UCLA
Extension's prestigious Writers' Program, where she
finally gets to utilise the MA and PhD in English
Literature that she received from the University of
York in England. She currently lives in the Pacific
Northwest, with her very own hero and too many
pets. Visit her at caitlincrews.com.

If you liked *Unleashed* why not try

UNLEASHED

CAITLIN CREWS

MILLS & BOON

First Published in Great Britain 2018
by Mills & Boon, an imprint of HarperCollins*Publishers*
1 London Bridge Street, London, SE1 9GF

© 2018 Caitlin Crews

ISBN: 978-0-263-93236-2

MIX
Paper from
responsible sources
FSC® C007454

This book is produced from independently certified FSC™ paper
to ensure responsible forest management.
For more information visit www.harpercollins.co.uk/green.

Printed and bound in Spain
by CPI, Barcelona

To Iceland, the most magical place I've ever been.

CHAPTER ONE

"I'M SORRY," THE overly polite receptionist said from behind the polished surface of the gleaming marble desk in Hotel Viking's iconic lobby. "The weather has turned foul. There will be no possibility of returning to Reykjavík tonight."

Professor Margot Cavendish squared her shoulders as if the woman had taken a swing at her, and forced a smile. It wouldn't do to let her irritation get the better of her, especially when she was mostly—okay, entirely—annoyed with herself.

She'd seen the weather with her very own eyes. She'd known that coming all the way out to this remote village was a risk, especially when there'd been no indication that the man she'd come to see would take a few minutes out of his busy schedule of sin and temptation to meet with her. He hadn't condescended to answer her emails or bothered to return her calls. And yet she'd gone ahead and come all this way anyway.

This was what she got for being spontaneous, she told herself darkly.

"It was snowing on the way here," she said, as if she could argue her way back to the little flat she was renting in central Reykjavík during her semester sabbatical. "It was a little slippery, but fine."

That wasn't entirely true. The road over the mountains had been treacherous. The snow had been coming down much harder up high than it had been in the city. But her taxi driver had been undeterred. And Margot was used to blustery Midwest winters at the University of Iowa, where she'd taught in the humanities department since completing her doctorate a few years back.

She wasn't afraid of a little snow. But she'd never spent a winter this close to the arctic, either.

"It's a developing storm, I'm afraid." The woman typed ferociously on her keyboard as if she was transmitting that same information to the public as she spoke. The tag on her chest read *Freyja*. "These winter storms are so unpredictable. It might very well clear up by morning."

"By morning?"

Margot's voice was too loud in the hushed, expensive lobby, which made her want to cringe. There was something about this place that got under her skin: its epic pageant of ice and fire on display wherever she went; elves and trolls and sagas wherever she looked, in one form or another. Like this hotel, a monument to sin that its reclusive owner somehow made seem attractive when Margot thought it should all be seedy. She could imagine the sort of things that must go on here, even if she hadn't seen much of it besides this damned lobby.

She forced her shoulders down an inch from where they'd crept up toward her ears. "You can't be suggesting I stay here overnight?"

She might or might not have emphasized the word *here* a bit too much.

The previous owner of the famous Hotel Viking, larger-than-life Daniel St. George, had died in a dramatic car accident in Germany some months before. His will had divided up his boutique hotel properties to the sons it had always been rumored he'd littered about the globe, though he'd never acknowledged them while alive. One of those assets had been Hotel Viking, the remote Icelandic hotel and resort that billed itself as the first and last stop in international fantasy. And it was only a couple of hours outside Reykjavík in good weather, so Margot had decided she had to go see it for herself.

Her current research project was all about Iceland and its reputation as the most feminist country in the world. Specifically, she was interested in sex and how Iceland's famous and highly alcoholic hookup culture intersected with those feminist principles— because to Margot's mind, those things didn't go together. She'd been in Reykjavík for almost a month already, consulting with colleagues at the University of Iceland and conducting interviews with as many locals as she could convince to talk with her on any given late night out there on Laugavegur—the famous street where so much of Reykjavík's nightlife happened—as they stumbled from bar to nightclub in the cold.

The name that kept cropping up was Thor Ragnarsson, the brand-new owner of the iconic Hotel Viking and the eldest of Daniel St. George's sons and heirs. Thor, who they whispered personally practiced all the many wicked things his guests got up to at the hotel. Thor, who seemed to embody all the things Margot liked least about men—in bed and out.

Overtly sexual. Too physical.

Not that it mattered what kind of sex the man had in his private life, of course. Margot wanted to know what he thought about sex in general, that was all.

Of course that was all. Even if she was trapped here.

His secretary had politely refused all requests for an interview when Margot had started calling instead of emailing. So she'd decided to just show up today and see what happened.

But she hadn't gotten past the lobby. Freyja had been polite but firm. The hotel proper was accessible only to its guests because complete privacy was its central promise, and Mr. Ragnarsson was unavailable for even a five-minute chat. It had been foolish for Margot to come here.

And now she had to pay for it.

"There are worse places to be snowed in," Freyja was saying. "After all, we're a hotel. There are those who get stuck in the snow out on the roads in these conditions and must hope for rescue."

"Yes, but…"

"Why don't you go and sit in our bar," Freyja suggested. "Have a drink. Relax. And I'll see how we can accommodate you tonight."

It wasn't as if Margot had a choice. She could see the way the snow was beating down outside. It swirled around on the other side of the glass entry doors with visibility of about an inch, leaving her well and truly trapped. She'd let herself grow complacent this past month in Reykjavík, clearly. She'd imagined that she could handle the snow the way the locals seemed to so easily.

And it had certainly never occurred to her that she could find herself stranded in a sex hotel. The whole building felt swollen with dark passions, with an undercurrent of sensuality weaving in and around everything, even the cheerful flower arrangements that adorned all the tables.

It was…disconcerting.

Margot had always viewed her body as an afterthought. She was a woman of intellect, not rampant, unchecked desires. She liked sex the way anyone did. Meaning, she enjoyed it. At its best it was fun. But she didn't *hunger* for it. She certainly wouldn't check into a special hotel to have particular kinds of operatic sex—mostly because she didn't like opera that much when it was sung, much less acted out in the flesh.

But Margot kept her thoughts on sex hotels and operas to herself. She nodded stiffly at Freyja, then made her way from the reception desk across the lobby toward the great, high doors on the far side that looked like they belonged on a Viking longhouse and led into the bar.

Hotel Viking was beautiful, as befit the exorbitant cost of even a single night's stay. It married the typical Scandinavian starkness of this part of the world with opulent details better suited to something more traditionally European and decadent, and somehow made it all work. And Margot found the hotel itself seemed to soothe her as she walked, not unlike a cool caress from a—

Get a grip, she ordered herself. She was not going to succumb to the sensual promise of this place. She wasn't a guest here. She didn't need a pageant with her orgasm when she could come happily and quickly and move on. She was an academic observer, that was all.

And she didn't like the fact she had to remind herself of that.

Almost as if she was afraid of what would hap-

pen if she surrendered to this place. As if the lure
of it was that powerful, even while she was doing
nothing more salacious than walking across a lobby.

Margot dismissed that notion almost in the same
instant. She wasn't *afraid*. She was a tenured professor back home, a position that had required single-
minded determination to achieve. She was a strong
and capable woman, wholly self-reliant, to the point
that her two last attempts at relationships had com-
plained bitterly about her independence on their way
out the door.

Good riddance, Margot had thought, once the
sting of each departure had faded. Because she
didn't believe that independence was anything to
be ashamed of.

And she certainly didn't think that finding herself
snowed in for the night in a sex hotel was any reason
to fear she might lose that independence.

Annoyed with herself, she pushed through the dou-
ble doors that looked like something out of *Beowulf*
and walked into the bar. She couldn't remember a
time she'd ever needed a glass of wine more.

Inside, it was far more ornate than the lobby. Deep
reds and golds somehow merged with a kind of in-
dustrial feel that, once again, shouldn't have worked
as well as it did. The light was dim and suggestive.
There were seats grouped together in intimate little
clusters, taking advantage of the deep shadows. Un-
earthly Icelandic music played while various configu-

rations of hotel guests talked. Flirted. And maybe did more than that under the stout wooden tables where no one could see.

Stop seeing sex everywhere, she ordered herself.

Margot ordered a drink from the friendly bartender and carried a gratifyingly large glass of wine to a little booth facing the windows on the far side of the bar, where she couldn't begin to figure out the relationships on display at all the other tables even if she wanted to. Instead, she had a front-row seat to the storm wreaking havoc outside.

Every now and again she saw glimpses of the surging sea far below, pounding against the obsidian volcanic rock the way it had done forever on this remote, northern island. But everything else was the snow. The wind rattled the windows, but it wasn't threatening now that she was sunk deep into a comfortable seat, safe and warm.

And yet a kind of threat seemed to roll over her anyway, making her skin prickle.

"Excuse me, I—"

Margot stiffened. She lifted a hand without looking up, stopping whatever was happening before it started.

"Thank you," she said coolly. "But I'd prefer to be alone."

"You are trapped in an isolated hotel in the middle of a blizzard," came the amused, decidedly male voice again, English spoken with an Icelandic accent that kicked its way down her spine like another caress. "It would be difficult to find more solitude than that."

"I understand that this is a sex hotel," she said crisply. She turned as she spoke, twisting around in her seat. And then looked up. And up further. And then still further, until she found the face of the man towering over her like a Viking god of old. "But I'm afraid I'm not a sex tourist. I'm just an accidental visitor."

The man standing beside her seat laughed. Loudly and deeply, as if he might break the windows in another moment if he let himself go. And Margaret was surprised to discover that his laughter seemed to move in her, too. It washed down her back, then spiraled even lower, settling like a fierce heat between her legs.

"This isn't a brothel," he said, all that laughter a kind of honey in his voice, and pooling in her, too. It made her feel almost…sticky. It made her very nearly wish that she really was a guest like everyone else. Like him. "What dark tales have you been reading?"

"The reputation of the Hotel Viking speaks for itself."

Margot was used to traveling alone. It rarely took more than a few cool words and an unapproachable expression on her face to deter unwanted male advances. Especially in Iceland, which prided itself

on its civility. But the man standing over her was...
different, somehow.

He was so big, for a start. Iceland was filled with
tall men, broad of shoulder and long of leg as befit
the descendants of Viking raiders. This man was all
that, but something else besides. Something *more*.
Every inch of him was packed with lean muscle, as
if he carried a leashed danger in every sinew and
held it in through sheer force of will.

And yet the way he stood there was easy. Lazy,
almost.

Margot was meant to be a clear-eyed observer of
humanity in all its complexities, damn it, so she was
forced to acknowledge the simple fact that this man
was easily the most striking she'd ever seen. He was
beautiful, in fact. His hair was a tawny gold, worn in
a careless length that looked as if he spent his days
raking his fingers through it—or more likely letting
others do that for him, if he spent time here.

And he had the face of a saint.

Nordic cheekbones. A carnal mouth.

And eyes so blue they burned.

Good lord, she burned.

"Exactly what have you heard about the hotel?"
he asked in that same boneless, effortlessly suggestive way.

Margot tried to school her expression to her usual
academic disinterest, but she couldn't quite get there.
Her pulse seemed to be everywhere, too hard and

too fast. She fingered the stem of her wineglass and sat back in her chair, hoping she looked as irritated as she wished she felt.

"The hotel is the premier international destination for extremely high-class pursuits of pleasure," she said, well aware that she was practically quoting from the website. "In whatever form they might take."

"Perhaps you misunderstand the word *pleasure*," he replied, but Margot doubted it. Not when she was looking at his mouth, hard and sensual. "A 'sex hotel' suggests a certain lack of consent. Prostitutes, for example. There's none of that here. The Hotel Viking caters to consenting adults."

"And of course there are no blurred lines," Margot said, as if she was auditioning to be a Puritan, all pursed lips and clutched pearls, when all she really wanted to know was how he made the word *consent* sound so hot. "Not in such a fine establishment as this."

"Some lines are better blurred." There was a gleam in the wild blue of his eyes that made her think of the northern lights that danced in the skies here, unworldly and impossible all at once. "But lines are not laws. Laws, you will find, are taken very seriously here."

She felt breathless, which was ridiculous. As if something about the simple fact of this man standing next to her table had reached inside her and scraped her hollow. Margot felt something like…jittery.

It was the storm, she told herself. The unpleasant novelty of finding herself stranded when she couldn't fix it. She couldn't walk away. She couldn't simply call a cab. There was no amount of intellect or cash that could beat back the snow.

Of course she didn't like it.

Margot told herself that was why she was reacting to this man the way she was. As if he was electric, when she didn't believe in that kind of thing. She didn't want it—it was messy and she hated opera and she had no interest in sex hotels on remote Icelandic peninsulas. She had too much work to do.

It was more than time to send him on his way. "It wouldn't matter if this was a convent. I'm not interested."

He laughed again, louder and longer than before. And once again, Margot could feel it everywhere, licking all over her like flames against her skin.

"I admire a woman who speaks her mind so distinctly. So there can be no mistake. You would be surprised how many people do not possess that particular talent."

"And yet here you still are."

"Forgive me," the man said, and that mouth of his curved into a smile that Margot absolutely did not feel directly in her breasts. Or in between her legs. Because she liked sex that was fun while it was happening but didn't interrupt her life afterward. Or even her schedule. She did not like…this. "I didn't come over here to ask you for a quick little fuck while the snow rages down, as diverting as that sounds. I am Thor Ragnarsson. I believe you're here to see me."

He pulled out the seat beside her and settled himself into it, while Margot couldn't seem to do a single thing but stare in shock.

Her heart was pounding in her chest, and her mind was spinning, desperately trying to figure out how she hadn't recognized him, while her body was getting a little too…operatic for her peace of mind. It was the angle, maybe. She'd seen pictures of him straight on, not from below, looking up. She might as well have been kneeling before him, head tipped back to receive his cock—

She sat up straighter, ignoring the fact her ears felt red and singed with the force of her embarrassment.

It had to be embarrassment that made her flush like that. It couldn't be anything else.

"Yes," she said, stiffly, casting around for her lost professionalism. "Mr. Ragnarsson, of course. I've been trying—"

"This is Iceland. We are not so formal. Call me Thor."

He was watching her intently and she told herself that was why his name seemed to sit there on her tongue like sugar. It wasn't an unusual name, not here. But there was something about him that made her think less of Icelandic naming traditions and a whole lot more about his namesake. The god of thunder.

The god of sex, they'd called him back in Reykjavík, with those suggestive little laughs.

She fought back a little shudder.

"Thor, then," she corrected herself. "I've emailed and left a number of messages. I am—"

"I know who you are. The American professor who wants to talk about sex."

There was no reason that should have sounded the way it did—intimate, suggestive—when it was the simple truth.

"Sex in a cultural sense, not a personal one," she clarified. "In case that's unclear."

His mouth curved again and its effect was even more pronounced when she was this close to him, tucked away in these high-backed chairs that concealed them from the rest of the bar. It was impossible not to notice how beautiful he was, there next to the howling storm outside. As if they were made of the same fury.

"Noted," he said, those eyes lit with suppressed laughter.

And something else she chose to ignore, because it felt a little too much like a kind of aria, lighting her up from the inside out.

Margot fumbled with her bag, reaching for her

notebook. "I have some questions to ask you. I'm mostly interested in how you think this hotel complicates the feminist reputation of Iceland's women, particularly in a sexual sense."

But when she wrestled her notebook to the table and looked up again, Thor was only sitting there in the same lazy way, studying her as if she fascinated him. As if she was the subject under consideration, not him.

Which she should not have found at all sexy.

"That is a very boring question."

She'd been staring at his mouth, so it took too long to process his actual words. "I beg your pardon?"

"Is that really what you want to know? You could have put that in an email. Instead, you took it upon yourself to drive out from Reykjavík. You tried to argue your way past my reception desk. All this because you wanted to know such a tedious thing?"

There was something fluttering deep inside her, making her entirely too aware of the growing heat and softness between her legs.

"So your answer is that you find feminism silly?"

"Not at all. I celebrate it."

He lounged there in his seat as if it was a throne and she was entirely too aware of him. The way his shoulders fit in the jacket he wore over a T-shirt that clung to the sculpted planes of his chest. How very long his legs were, thrust out before him. The way his hands moved on the arms of his chair, his fingers long and clever. He looked like what he was: a very confident, even arrogant man, who clearly imagined himself the winner in any game he chose to play.

But Margot had never been very good at losing.

"How exactly do you celebrate feminism?" she asked, her gaze steady on his, because she was the professor and he was the pervert, no matter the odd little scenarios that kept playing on repeat in her head. If she really did kneel. If he moved a little closer, here where no one could see. If he pressed into her from behind, her skin flushed and hot against the cold glass of the windows… But she had to stop this madness. "Is it by throwing one of your sex parties?"

"There's nothing I love more than a woman who knows her own mind and every inch of her own body," Thor told her, his teeth flashing in a grin that was much too dangerous for a man who looked so at his ease. Or maybe it was just too dangerous for her, because she couldn't seem to breathe past it. "I find nothing sexier than equality, particularly in bed."

It took everything Margot had not to squirm in her seat. She didn't want to think about him in bed.

And she couldn't seem to think about anything else.

"By your response, am I to assume that you think feminism is a sexual act?"

"It is when I do it," he said, amusement flickering over his face. "But perhaps not for you, of course. You have my condolences."

"I would prefer if you keep things professional," she said, but for the first time in her academic life, she wasn't sure that was true.

"I know all about your research, Dr. Cavendish," he said, and Margot was certain she detected a mocking inflection to the way he said her name. Because, of course, Icelanders did not use titles or even surnames for that matter. "I've been receiving reports of you almost from the very moment you set foot on our little volcanic island."

Margot frowned. "Reports?"

"If it had appeared that your questions bothered my customers, I would have had to encourage you to conduct your experiments elsewhere. You understand."

Margot's frown deepened. "You can't think—"

"But all you have collected are stories."

There was something in the way he said that that made her stop protesting. She found herself leaning forward, as if compelled against her will, except that couldn't be right. Margot made it a point never to do a single thing she didn't want to do.

Did that mean she wanted this? Him?

Because when Thor smiled at her, all thunder and heat, she just wanted to melt.

"Have you ever asked yourself what would happen if you stopped recording secondhand stories and found out for yourself?" he asked idly.

Though there was nothing idle about the way he looked at her.

She sat straighter, because it was that or succumb to the madness coursing through her veins, making her imagine…all kinds of things. Operas and perversities, decadent and lush, and his hands all over her while they did them. "Let me guess. This is where you offer to get into my pants, for the good of my research."

"Icelanders fuck, Dr. Cavendish." He lounged there, as intent and watchful as he was boneless. "They do not waste all this time talking. Fuck first, then, if it is any good, perhaps talk a little. Haven't you already discovered this in all your research?"

She nodded, trying to pull herself together. "It's that exact permissiveness that interests me."

"There are some things that intellect cannot help you with. I think you'll find that sex is one of them."

Margot sat back in her chair. "I see no one has told you the most powerful sexual organ in a woman's body is her brain."

"You say that," Thor said, a rich vein of laughter in that deep voice of his. "But I've had a remarkable amount of success with the clit."

Which meant she could do nothing but feel that laughter in hers.

"Exactly what are you offering?" she asked, perhaps more harshly than necessary, crossing her legs against the intense throbbing sensation where she least wanted it. "If you wanted to hit on me, you should have said so from the start."

"This 'hitting' on you," he said, as if he was unfamiliar with the term. "As if attraction is an assault. Is that how you see sex? Is that an American thing—or is it you?"

Margot didn't like that his comment landed, hard. It made her feel a little dizzy. "It's a figure of speech."

"Surely an academic such as yourself loves nothing more than to dig her claws into figures of speech."

"Because you have a vast interest in academic pursuits, of course."

"In pursuits, yes. Not necessarily of the academic variety."

"They told me at the reception desk that I was trapped here for at least the night," Margot said crisply. "Possibly more than one night, if the storm rages on. Is this the price of a room? Sex with you?"

The amusement in his gaze shifted, growing darker and more focused at once. For a long moment, he didn't speak. He only watched her, and she thought she could see a muscle tense in his lean jaw.

Holding her gaze, Thor reached into the pocket of his jacket and drew out a key. It was an old-fashioned key with an exuberant flourish on its end. He placed it on the table between them with a decisive click.

"This is your room key," he told her quietly. She was riveted by the thunder that stormed around beneath those seemingly soft words. "There is no price. You may stay until the storm blows itself out, with my compliments."

"Did I… Did I offend you?" she asked, not certain why that possibility seemed to tilt madly inside her, as if she was on some kind of roller coaster.

"It is my mistake," Thor said with a faint smile. "This is a cultural thing, I think. Icelanders talk very openly about sex. Having it, not having it. Who they wish to have it or not have it with. Offers are made, accepted, rejected. This happens all the time. I would have thought you'd know this, given your field of study."

Once again, Margot felt off balance, and she hated it. "Is this the part where you try to make me feel bad, as if I'm somehow unsophisticated and re-pressed for calling you out?"

"You can call me whatever you wish," Thor said, his voice deeper, somehow. Or maybe that was just how it felt inside her, where her body was acting as if it belonged to someone else. Someone who wanted sex to be a whole lot more than *enjoyable*. "I do not require payment for kindness. It insults me that you might think otherwise, but I understand. You come from a place where sexual politics are significantly more adversarial. You cannot help but fight, no mat-ter what it is that you want."

Margot didn't know which was drier, her lips or

her throat. Especially when he shrugged as if she was that easily summarized. That easily understood.

"And I suppose you're here to tell me what it is that I want?"

"I don't think it's accidental that you chose to come to my sex hotel." And the way he said those words, *sex hotel*, was like sharp blades. "On the day of a storm."

"You think I planned to strand myself in a snow-storm?" Margot laughed and told herself it wasn't the least bit forced. "For this? For you?"

He didn't laugh. "I like sex. I'm not afraid of it."

"I'm not afraid of sex."

But there was something in the denial that made her wish she could snatch the words back. Especially when his blue gaze seemed hotter. Wilder.

"Maybe you are and maybe you're not." He shrugged. "What I know about you is that you have done nothing but watch. What I can offer you is the opportunity to do a little fieldwork."

"Fieldwork?" She blinked. "Is that a joke?"

"I never joke," he said, deadpan. "I'm far too perverse. Do you need to get to know someone before you sleep with them?"

"You say that as if it's a bad thing."

"Not at all," Thor said. "But in Iceland, that's back to front. I could sit here and tell you my life story or you could come to my rooms with me and I will show you. It will be there in the chemistry between us, or not. Every answer to every question you have, laid out before you clearly and inarguably."

"Because you're that good in bed."

Thor laughed, though it was quieter than before. And somehow, she thought, more volatile. "I don't believe in 'good in bed.' Either people connect or they don't. One woman's sex god is another's dud. It is all chemistry."

"What if we have no chemistry?"

He smiled at that and it felt like fire. Then he leaned forward, putting his hand on the table, his palm up.

"Maybe we don't." He nodded at his hand. "Why don't you touch me and see."

Margot ordered herself to remain calm. She couldn't remember the last time a man had tied her into knots the way this one was doing so effortlessly.

Was that chemistry? Or was she in over her head with this latter-day Viking?

This was her opportunity to put them back on proper footing. Before things spiraled even further out of control.

But Margot wasn't one to back down from a challenge. Instead of turning it over and over in her head the way she probably should have, she leaned forward and slid her hand over his.

She expected him to be strong. For his hand to be warm and to envelop hers the way it did. But the contact jolted through her like a flash of lightning, and she had to bite back the involuntary little noise she made.

Not that it mattered. She could see from the burning thing in his gaze that he felt it, too. And more, that he had heard her.

As if he could feel that same lightning. As if it crackled in them both.

"Here is your opportunity to be less American and more Icelandic," Thor said, his voice rougher than before. Lower. "You've been trying to talk to me for weeks now. This is your opportunity."

"You're not offering to talk."

"Oh, don't worry," Thor murmured. His palm slid against hers as he flipped her hand over. "I'm fluent in all kinds of languages."

Margot fought the urge to yank her hand away from his. Because there was too much sensation, suddenly. Because she'd completely lost control of this interaction. Because there was a part of her that didn't quite know what to do with all the wild things she could feel storming around inside her, competing with the swirling snow outside the windows.

Be practical, she ordered herself. *Think this through.*

It was unorthodox, certainly. But she would be lying if she tried to pretend that she hadn't wondered what it would be like to be one of those Icelandic girls, casual in ways she had never quite managed to be.

Margot had never had sex with a stranger. She wasn't the kind of woman men tended to pick up in bars. Because she was generally unimpressed with drunken attempts at conversation. And because she preferred to spend her time in libraries and class-rooms. The men in her life had always been like her, academic and intellectual and more interested in an intense conversation than sex.

Not so intensely physical and overwhelming that she'd forgotten they weren't alone in the room.

Maybe it was time to see what all the fuss was about. And who better than Iceland's god of sex?

"It would be for research purposes only," she heard herself say.

Thor's impossibly carnal mouth curved. But his eyes were like flame. "Of course."

"Just sex," Margot said. "And only during the storm."

"If you insist."

"I do insist." There was something about the way he was regarding her then, leashed and ready, as if he knew something she didn't. As if he knew her better than she knew herself, which Margot didn't like at all, no matter how wet the notion made her. "And no kissing."

She wasn't sure he would agree to that, and the more she stared at his mouth, the more she won-dered why she'd said it in the first place. Because the urge to lean forward then, to crawl across the table between them and set her mouth to his, was nearly overwhelming.

But that half smile of his only deepened.

"No kissing," he agreed.

"Great," she said brightly, as if they were discussing the kind of sex she studied, not the kind she was going to have. "I'm sure one round with the self-styled king of fantasy will be a perfect experiment."

Thor took his time standing up from his chair. He didn't let go of her hand, so Margot found herself standing with him. For a moment it was awkward, and then he pulled her toward him until she was *this close* to falling against his big, broad chest.

And worse, wanted to.

"I do love an experiment," he said, in a kind of drawl, all command and blue fire. "But prepare yourself, Professor, because it won't be just once."

CHAPTER TWO

THE PROFESSOR HAD purple hair.

Well, it was more properly a deep lavender. It cascaded over her shoulders and caught the light, and was almost impossible not to reach out and touch.

But he managed it.

It wasn't as if Thor had never seen brightly colored hair on a woman before. Still, he had never met a woman so determined to present herself as profoundly serious while supporting such...unserious hair.

The contrast intrigued him.

But then, everything about Margot Cavendish was intriguing.

Why had she come all the way to his hotel in the middle of a storm, for example, only to pretend that it was some kind of accident? It wasn't as if Thor was a hermit. He made it into Reykjavík often. It would have been easy enough for this American professor to camp out in one of his city clubs if she really wanted to run into him.

Thor did not believe in accidents. He'd been running Hotel Viking for almost six months now, ever since the man he did not consider his father in any real sense had left it to him in that odd will. The same will that had also presented Thor with two half brothers he'd never met—and wasn't sure he wanted to know. And one thing he'd learned in his months as the proprietor of the world's finest and most remote purveyor of fantasies was that no one rolled up to this place by accident.

Oh, they might tell themselves otherwise. They might make up all kinds of stories to convince themselves they hadn't meant to come here. As if it was possible to accidentally end up in Iceland. Or to take a wrong turn in the middle of Reykjavík and end up hours away on a lonely little peninsula that was near absolutely nothing but the pitiless sea.

It never took long to reveal that, in point of fact, they'd been heading for Hotel Viking all along.

Thor led the prickly, lavender-haired professor out of his sumptuous bar, built to be an endless celebration of luxurious sin. He nodded at the bartender as he went, smiling when he saw that one of the guests—a Mr. Oliveras from Portugal—was chatting Kristjan up.

"Do you let your employees date your guests?" his professor asked as they passed.

Thor was fairly certain that was a touch of judgment he heard in her tone. But that wouldn't surprise him. Thor had yet to meet an American—no matter how supposedly liberal—who didn't carry that country's moralistic roots inside themselves somewhere.

He allowed that he found that just as fascinating, having not a shred of the puritanical anywhere in him. At all.

"Some establishments that cater to the kinds of sexual fantasies we do have all kinds of draconian regulations about the behavior of staff toward guests, but Hotel Viking isn't one of them." Thor smiled down at her and wondered why he so badly wanted to taste that intriguing little furrow between her eyes as she frowned at him, very obviously *thinking* at him. "Our staff are encouraged to follow their passions as they like."

"That sounds problematic."

"Only if you find happy, satisfied and loyal employees problematic. I do not."

He kept one hand in the small of Margot's back as he moved her through the big bar doors and back into the gleaming lobby, as much to maintain contact with her as to guide her anywhere.

And also because he suspected any hint of chivalry would irritate her. The more irritated she was, the more likely she was to stay off balance.

And Thor had a powerful urge to rattle this woman, just a little. Just enough. To peel away her composure and see beneath it.

He had thought she was attractive from the first

moment he'd laid eyes on her, stalking across his hotel and then sitting as far away as it was possible to get from the place while still being in it. But it was something else again to talk with her.

Especially when she'd been so committed to shutting down what she'd seen as his unwelcome advances. Thor couldn't remember the last time he'd been rejected. He'd enjoyed the experience, if he was honest.

And he'd enjoyed her.

Thor liked her brain—especially when he could *see* her using it.

At him.

He'd always had a thing for smart women, but he found himself particularly intrigued by Margot, who seemed to be so delightfully unaware of her own body's needs and the way she was broadcasting them. He could feel her anticipation even now. It was like a hum just beneath her skin and he could feel it in the fingertips that grazed her back.

Thor led her across the lobby, smiling at Freyja behind the main desk, and headed for his private elevator far in the corner.

"Let me guess. You're taking me to your dungeon."

Thor studied Margot as they stepped into the lift and she put as much distance between them as it was possible to get in such a small, enclosed space.

"I can tell that you are joking," he said after a moment. "But perhaps not entirely joking, yes?"

"Of course I'm joking." She sounded fierce. But Thor noticed that it wasn't until the elevator doors were closed behind them and the lift moved upward that she released the breath she was holding. Her shoulders inched down from around her ears.

"Professor, you must trust me on this, if nothing else," he murmured, enjoying himself far more than he should. "You are in no way ready for the dungeon."

He was fascinated anew by the flush that stained her cheeks and swept down her neck. And the suggestion of heat—and a thousand questions—in her gaze.

And more than all that, the fact she didn't reply.

Thor felt certain that her silence said a great deal more than she likely wished to reveal.

"Why no kissing?" he asked mildly as the lift rose, slow and steady. He lounged across from her, crossing his arms and his legs at the ankle as if they were off to discuss something prosaic. Numbers, perhaps. Or taxes.

Margot frowned. "You agreed."

He couldn't quite hide his smile. "I agreed, yes. I'm wondering why."

"Because it made more sense that way." She blinked, as if she hadn't wanted to say that. Or not quite that way. "Kissing is too…"

"Intimate?"

He watched another flush of color move over her face, deeper this time, making an interesting counterpoint to the lavender of her hair. It made her look prettier, though that shouldn't have been possible. It made her look delicate, and oddly young in contrast to the scowling severity she had exuded down at the bar.

And he felt that like a long, hot lick down the length of his cock.

"Kissing is something you do in a relationship," Margot declared as if she had a doctorate in the subject. It was possible she did. "It has no place in this sort of arrangement."

"You say that with great authority. Have you had many such arrangements?"

"We already agreed that this is for research, Mr.—" She stopped herself. "*Thor.* There's no need to confuse the issue."

He shrugged. "I cannot say that I have ever found kissing confusing."

"You also consider sex to be about as intimate as a handshake. It's possible that you're not really the ideal control group for this experiment."

That amused him. "I can tell the difference between sex and a handshake."

He wondered if she realized that she had crossed her arms over her chest, too. Mirroring him, perhaps. Or Thor supposed it was possible she was simply naturally defensive. Either way, that awkward bristling, endearing as it was, melted away the more professorial she got.

He filed that away.

"You said downstairs that you get to know people through sex."

"There is little that's more revealing. I mean that literally, of course." His mouth curved. "As the participants are usually naked."

"And modesty is not a huge concern here, is that right?"

"It is my belief that false modesty has no place anywhere," Thor replied. "But Icelanders spend a lot of time in the baths, as I'm sure you know. We are used to seeing all sorts of different body shapes. It is not like America, where you are bombarded with images of unhealthy bodies constantly. It's a wonder that Americans ever take their clothes off at all."

Margot nodded as if he'd confirmed something for her. "So your position is that sex ought to be as casual as a trip to the hot tub. And you would prefer to start with sex rather than beginning with a coffee or a dinner date, which I'm sure you know is more common in other countries."

He laughed. "It must surely be far more awkward to share a meal with someone who, for all you know, will completely fail to satisfy you in any way sexually. Why waste all that time?"

Thor was being somewhat facetious. But there was something about the way she frowned at him. There was something about the way her theories seemed broadcast across her face. He could *see* her turn over the things she thought, one after the next. He wasn't entirely sure why he thought it was so hot.

And why not play into her ideas about their cultural differences? She wasn't entirely wrong. Thor had spent a very informative year in America when he'd been of university age. He had been amazed at the gulf between the permissiveness of the American media, in all its forms—like bikini-clad models on hand to sell a hamburger—and the actual behavior of its citizens in private.

"Do you consider yourself a sexual libertine?" she asked him, in a matter-of-fact tone of voice, as if the word *libertine* was one people usually threw about so casually in conversation.

"Are you asking for personal reasons, given what we're about to do? Or is this more of your general research?"

"Research. Of course."

"I have been called many things in my time," Thor replied. And then laughed. "Why do you ask?"

"Yours was the name that came up repeatedly while I was doing interviews on Laugavegur. I'm trying to decide if you're different from the average Icelander or if you're a decent representative of Icelandic mores."

"I consider myself a unique little snowflake, of course."

"Well, there are a lot of those in Iceland," she said. She smiled. "Snowflakes, I mean."

Thor liked that. He liked the glint of challenge in her hazel eyes that looked gold in the elevator light. And he was looking forward to getting his hands in all that hair.

"There is a great deal of snow in Iceland, it is true. Just as I believe there are a legion or two of purple-haired women in your precise demographic. Is that not so?"

Margot reached up and tugged on a strand of her hair. "I like it."

"But why do you like it?" Thor asked, mildly enough. "Isn't this the sort of thing you study? Why it is that certain habits or choices—casual sex, let us say, or the sudden rise of purple-haired women— suddenly sweep the planet?" He studied her as she stared back at him. "Perhaps we all like what we like, Professor."

He wasn't sure she liked that too much, but then they arrived. The elevator doors opened smoothly and delivered them directly into the owner's penthouse that rambled over the entire top floor of the hotel.

Thor walked in, turning on a light here and there as he went. He didn't look back to see if Margot was following him. He didn't have to. He could hear her feet in her heavy winter boots on his blond wood floors.

"This is…" He could hear the nerves in her voice, making her sound huskier than before. It made him that much harder. "Stark."

"Nordic, I think you mean."

"This seems excessively Nordic."

Thor stopped in the center of the vast living room and looked around. It was all open space, exposed steel beams and floor-to-ceiling windows that let the best and worst of the weather in. The furniture was low and spare with a modern edge. Geometric shapes, designed to make the most of the space and to enjoy what little light there was for half the year. The living area was designed to feel three times its size, and it did. But then, Thor was a very large man, a credit to his Viking forebears. He wasn't fond of tight, cramped little spaces with low ceilings and no air.

"The rest of the hotel veers toward the lush," he said, looking back at her. "I prefer something a little more austere."

"Clearly." But she kept walking toward him, even though her arms were still crossed over her chest. "I imagine that tells me all kinds of things about you."

"That I am a product of my environment?"

"I was thinking more…lush in the streets and stark in the sheets."

Thor let out a laugh at that and watched Margot blink, as if she hadn't expected it.

"I don't think *stark* is the word, but you will have to let me know what you think after you've experienced my sheets, I think."

Thor led her all the way across the living room and then into the bedroom on the far side. It featured a wall of windows with mechanized shutters to keep out the white nights in summer, thick rugs on the floor, and his bed wasn't the least bit clean and spare. It was a towering four-poster monstrosity that looked as if it could entertain the entire hotel.

"Better?" he asked. "Less offensively Nordic?"

She stopped just inside the door and swallowed convulsively. He watched the way her throat moved and felt it ripple through him like some kind of honey.

He moved over to the wall that faced the bed and set about building a fire in the large fireplace that was set halfway up one wall, sleek and smooth.

By the time he had the flames crackling, Margot had inched a little bit farther into the room.

He took that as a good sign. "You look remarkably nervous for a little research trip."

"I'm not nervous at all."

"Professor." Thor was still squatting there before the fireplace. He turned without rising so he could keep his gaze trained on her. "This is not going to be very much fun if you lie to me."

Her brows drew together. "I'm not lying."

"Perhaps you do not mean to lie." He shook his head. "But look how you are standing. Stiff. Tense. Profoundly unwelcoming. What am I to make of this body language?"

"Why do you have to make something of it?"

"Margot." Thor liked the way she reacted to her

name in his mouth. He more than liked it. He felt the air between them ignite. "I am not in the habit of fucking women who look about as excited at the prospect as they might a trip to the dentist."

She actually jolted at that, then scowled, which he already understood was her natural progression in all things.

"You're reading me completely wrong." But her voice was flat, contradicting her own words.

Thor stayed where he was. "Am I?"

"I told you. This is supposed to be about research. And the research is not about me."

"You are the one doing the research," Thor pointed out. Patiently. "With me. And I prefer a little more enthusiasm. It is a requirement, in fact."

"I'm enthusiastic."

"You are quite obviously nothing of the kind."

"I don't think you have the slightest idea what you're talking about."

"Probably not." He lifted a brow. "Prove me wrong, then."

He wasn't sure what Margot would do. But then again, that was precisely why these situations fascinated him. How better to know a person than to see what they would do in unforeseen, fraught circumstances?

Thor shifted back on his heels and stayed where he was. He could stay there all night, watching Margot *think*.

And he wondered what it would be like to know her better, to be able to tell what sort of thoughts they were that made her frown like that; that made those clever eyes of hers glitter.

She pressed her lips together as if she was girding her loins for a potentially unpleasant task, and then she marched toward the huge bed.

When she reached it, she threw a look at him as if she expected him to comment on what she was doing, but Thor only smiled. And waited.

Margot tossed her coat onto the leather chair next to the bed. She threw her bag down beside it. She did both with a level of aggression that Thor would have laughed at, had he not felt the moment was perhaps a little fragile.

So he said nothing. He waited.

Holding his gaze, Margot sat down on the edge of the chair and began to work at the laces of her boots. They were the high kind, with fur around the tops, and it took her a moment to loosen each side, then pull her leg out.

Again, she looked at Thor as she took each boot off and set it beside the chair with a certain ferocious precision.

And again, he only watched. And kept his own counsel.

"Are you just going to sit there?" she demanded.

"I am," he replied. "I don't think it's *my* enthusiasm that requires proof, is it? After all, I'm the reason we're here and not exchanging barbs and very little wine down in the bar."

"You're the one who said consent was sexy."

"I beg your pardon." He kept his gaze on hers, steady. Demanding. And had the great pleasure of watching that telling flush move over her face. "Do you not find me sexy?"

She didn't answer him with words. But there was no noise in the room, save the crack and pop of the fire, and so he heard the breath she let out. In a rush.

Thor felt that was answer enough.

Her chin tipped up in another show of whatever this was. Aggression. Nerves.

Or, something in him murmured, *how little she knows her own desires.*

His were far more straightforward and he wasn't in any doubt about them. He wanted to get inside her. He wanted her astride him, that lavender hair cascading all over the both of them as she rode him. He wanted his hands on her breasts and he wanted to hear what she sounded like when she came.

The sooner, the better.

She held his gaze then, steady and sure, which he doubted she knew was perhaps the sexiest thing she could do.

Her hands were busy with her clothes. She pulled off the jumper she wore, a thin merino wool. Then the base layer she wore beneath it. She stood there a moment, as if reveling in the fact that she was standing in front of a stranger wearing nothing but a pale blue lace bra that cupped a good-sized pair of breasts, round and plump. Her waist nipped in, then out again, to the flare of her hips.

Thor's mouth watered.

He let his gaze track over her. He estimated she was around five feet seven, and she wasn't skinny. She had the sort of athletic build that Thor liked best—muscled, capable and solid. She looked like a woman who could walk anywhere, hike a mountain if she felt like it and then spend a long, hot night with a lover.

Perfect, in other words, for a man like Thor, who liked to sweat in a variety of settings.

When he didn't say anything, Margot went to work on her trousers. She pulled off what looked like snow pants, revealing another base layer. When she pulled that off, too, she worked her socks off at the same time, and then he watched as she carefully, ferociously, folded every item she'd peeled off and set it on the chair in a ruthlessly neat little pile.

And then his professor with the magical hair turned back around and stood before him in only her bra and a surprisingly suggestive pair of thong panties in a bright pink leopard print.

Thor's mouth went dry.

Her legs were as lean and muscular as the rest of her, and long enough to give him particularly bright fantasies of how they would feel looped over his shoulders.

"Well?" she asked. In her voice that was both huskier than before and more than a little belligerent. "Are you satisfied?"

"That you know how to remove your clothes?" He did nothing to keep the amusement from his voice. Or the heat. "Yes, I am satisfied. But if this is enthusiasm, Professor, I am tempted to imagine you do not know the meaning of the word."

The look she gave him then was something like murderous, so Thor wasn't sure why it made him want to laugh. He thought better of it.

Margot made a frustrated sort of noise in the back of her throat. Then she moved again, unbuckling her bra and throwing it on the chair beside her. Then she hooked her fingers in her panties and tugged them down her legs, before kicking them off.

Then she was naked.

And it was like the blizzard that raged just there outside his windows disappeared. As if the world narrowed to this single woman in this shadowy room lit by the fire.

He took a long moment to appreciate the way she gleamed while the firelight licked and danced over her lean curves and gently sculpted limbs—and to make sure he was completely in control of himself despite the storm of need that pounded through him.

She was pale. She had a tattoo that wrapped

around her left side, a series of typewritten words declaring her persistence. She wore a little silver ring in her navel.

And in between her legs was a triangle of strawberry blond curls.

Thor felt his pulse batter at him. In his temples. His chest. His heavy cock. He took his time lifting his gaze to hers again.

"Is that your natural hair color?"

"That's a personal question," she retorted.

"It was a rhetorical question. I feel certain nature did not gift you with purple hair, no matter how, exactly, you persist."

Her hazel eyes looked like dark gold coins in the firelight. And they narrowed as she stared at him.

"Yes," she said stiffly. "Sometimes I'm a redhead."

Thor stood then. He was aware of the way she tracked his every movement. The way her gaze dropped to play over his chest. Then bounced back up to his face again, as if she felt guilty for taking pleasure in him.

"Explain to me what is intimate and what is not, please," he said as he moved toward her. Slowly. Almost lazily. "You do not wish to kiss on the mouth. But you're already naked. Your nudity is not intimate, but a question about hair color is?"

She scowled at him. He didn't know why he found that…delightful.

"We're supposed to be having sex," she said, her

voice ripe with impatience. "Not playing these ridiculous 'get to know you' games."

"Oh, Professor," he murmured. "I haven't even begun to play games."

Margot breathed harder the closer he came. He liked it. It told him more things about her than he imagined she knew she was giving away, and he liked that, too. He moved over until he stood next to the bed, facing her.

Still holding her gaze, Thor reached out and patted the mattress beside him.

She swallowed again, visibly, and he watched in fascination as she fought with herself. He could actually see the fight. It was as obvious to him as if she was taking swings at herself.

Her fists clenched and released. Once, then again.

Then she moved, jerkily, and climbed up to sit on the very spot that he'd patted with his hand.

He moved so he was standing at the side of the bed, then. He moved himself between her legs so she was forced to open them even wider. Thor leaned forward, planting his hands on either side of her as she fell back, catching herself on her elbows.

He wasn't even touching her. But he could smell her arousal. He could see it in that telltale flush that moved down from her pretty face to cover the whole of her chest. Her breasts sloped slightly to the sides and the nipples were already pink and hard. Flushed, they seemed to gleam like heat.

She was breathing as if he was already inside her.

"Why is this a struggle for you?" he asked with deliberate politeness, as if he'd offered to call her a taxi.

"It's not a struggle at all."

"Liar."

That flush of hers got brighter. Redder.

"I don't know," she whispered.

"That's not good enough, Professor. Try again. Use that brain of yours."

"I've never done this before." She said it in a rush, as if it was a confession. "I've never— You're a stranger."

"You have researched me already. You know far more about me than if I was merely a stranger you met in a bar."

"I don't pick up strangers in bars."

"You didn't pick me up, either. It was quite the opposite, if you'll recall."

She stared at him a moment. Then that chin of hers tilted up again.

"Is this why you got me naked?" she demanded. "So we could talk?"

Thor laughed at that, and even that made his impatient cock ache. He shifted so he was leaning over her more, bearing her back against his bed.

"Remember," he told her sternly. "You're not allowed to kiss me no matter what happens. This is your rule."

She frowned at that, as he had known she would.

She was sucking in a breath, no doubt to share her indignation, when he dropped another inch and took one of those pink nipples in his mouth.

Finally.

And whatever she might have said was choked off. Then turned into a cute little sound of need that Thor liked.

A lot.

Margot moaned something, but he didn't pay attention to it.

He paid attention to her gorgeous body instead. He lavished that first nipple with attention, testing the lush, perfect shape of the other with his hand.

Then he switched places, and as he did, he learned her responses, her taste. The way she writhed beneath him, shifting her legs and lifting her hips. She slid down off her elbows and arched her back, offering him more of her.

More access. More of those hot little noises.

More.

But it got even better when she lifted her hands and sank them into his hair, not to stop him or guide him, but as if she couldn't help herself.

And after a while, Thor could feel the ache of his own need edging toward pain in his cock. But he didn't hurry anything along. He explored her, reveling in his own delayed gratification.

Because his ornery American was giving herself

to him, and he wanted to marinate in every single moment of it.

He moved from those velvety nipples down to her soft belly, where he amused himself with that belly ring of hers and her shuddery responses. He tested the span of her hips with his hands, and when he was tempted to bury his face between her legs and drink her down, he thought better of it.

For the moment.

He flipped her over onto her belly instead.

She made a low sound as he crawled up onto the bed and dropped down closer to her. He set his mouth behind her ear, then made his way to the nape of her neck.

He found that he could make her squirm.

And he did.

Thor followed a meandering path down the length of her spine, then made her shiver and buck a little when he found the sweet curve of her ass.

He let his thumbs graze that dark furrow and the sweeter heat beneath, but he didn't go deep.

He didn't know why he was restraining himself until she made a low, hot sound of protest. He grinned, then nipped at her nape, using his teeth lightly until she was shuddering all over again.

Only then did he turn her over yet again.

He ran his hands along her legs, enjoying the play of her quads and her calves. He found her ankles and then lifted her, draping her legs over his shoulders.

Margot was breathing fast then.

Heavy, hard.

And there was a wildness, a glorious heat, in her gaze that hadn't been there before.

He held her ass in his hands again, levering her up off the bed so she was at an angle.

And it was impossible not to notice that she was exactly the right size, scaled to fit him perfectly. He could lift her. He could play with her. And soon enough, he would be so deep inside her it would feel like coming home.

Thor was actually shaking a little, he wanted to fuck her so badly.

"I want to lick you until you scream," he told her, and his voice was gruff. He felt so greedy and insane with need. "It's my preferred version of a handshake."

"Oh my god."

"I am named for a god, it is true. Are you calling out my name, Professor? Or is that a prayer for deliverance?"

She sucked in a breath that sounded like a moan and writhed in his grip. Her hair was spread out around her, a bright tangle on the bed.

"Why are you talking about it?" she demanded, her eyes too dark and too gold, and furious. Thor could relate. "Why don't you just *do* it?"

"If you want me to do something, Margot," he told her, clipped and dark, "you need to ask for it. By name."

CHAPTER THREE

MARGOT'S ENTIRE BODY was rioting.

Everything seemed connected. Her breath. Her pulse. The wild heat that stormed through her and made her want to do things she couldn't even name—things she'd never thought she'd have the slightest interest in before tonight.

Before Thor.

She didn't understand what had happened. One moment she'd been in complete control. She'd been aware that he was baiting her, but that had been fine. She'd had more than a little anxiety about what she was planning to do, and the fact that Thor kept challenging her helped. She'd undressed as she wished, making certain that the entire exercise felt like what it was: work.

Then everything had shifted, rendering her something like drunk when she'd barely tasted her wine. But that was how it felt. The imposing walls of this penthouse of his had seemed to slip and slide, and the heated floor beneath her feet had seemed to buckle.

It was something about that arctic blue gaze of his

and the way he fixed it on her, as if he didn't care what that kind of intense focus might tell her about him. It was the way he'd stayed there, low before the fire as if he didn't hum with all that lethal energy and had done nothing but…watch.

Even thinking about it made her shudder where he held her, lifted up and off the bed though her shoulders were still pressed into the mattress.

And Thor was still dressed.

Somehow that made it all hotter. Dirtier. He was fully clothed while she writhed about, flushed red and naked and wide-open to him.

Imagining what she must look like to him made her shudder again, perilously close to another wild shattering.

"I don't beg," she panted out at him, trying to force a little more air into her chest.

The look on his face was too wicked to name.

"If you say so. But I did not ask you to beg. Just ask me for what you want, Margot. Ask me, or I will simply hold you here. Like this. Forever."

She believed him. She wasn't sure why, because it didn't make any sense that he would actually do something as ridiculous as what he'd threatened when the entire point of them being here was to have sex. Not stand around in odd positions.

But the truth was that her body didn't find anything about Thor ridiculous.

Not one thing. Not even his sensual threats.

She pushed herself up onto her elbows again. She told herself she was uncomfortable, that she was cold and in a strangely angled position—but even if that was true, she couldn't say she cared much.

Thor's hands were big like the rest of him, and he held her ass securely as if he really could do it forever. She felt almost as if he was burning her, his palms were so hot.

And her pussy was so wet it occurred to her that she ought to be embarrassed.

She told herself she wasn't, but a kind of electric shame flashed through her, telling her what a liar she was.

"I don't understand," she managed to say, though she could hardly hear her own voice over the roaring in her ears.

"You do."

"I don't see why I have to perform for you."

"You can either own your sexual desires or you can deny them," Thor said, that voice of his like gravel though it rolled through her like some kind of honey, pooling in all the dark places inside her she'd never acknowledged. "But only one of those things is going to get you off."

Something was building inside Margot then. It felt much too intense. It felt much too close, too scary—

But this is sex, she told herself. *It's just sex.*

And sex wasn't scary. It was sometimes awkward, or messy, or better in theory than in practice because penises never behaved as advertised and her own orgasm was often hard to chase down, but it wasn't *scary*.

Besides, she was here for research purposes. And there was nothing scary about research. Why was she psyching herself out?

"Put your mouth on me," she blurted out, and it was as if she'd stuck her hands into an electrical socket. Everything went white-hot inside her, all over her, until even her breath felt edgy. Raw.

"Where?" Thor's voice was stern. Implacable.

"I can't…"

"If you can't name it, Margot, how can you truly enjoy it?"

"This is no time for philosophy."

He didn't relent. "Where, Professor? Where do you want my mouth?"

She was wide-open before him. He was lifting her off the bed as if he was prepared to serve himself a taste of her—and she was bright and hot and shuddery at the very idea. Her pussy was melting and wild, with a dangerous pulse all its own.

And it wasn't as if the rest of her was any better.

Margot pressed her elbows down against the mattress beneath her. Her hands were in fists against the comforter. She was tense and needy, sensations she'd never felt in her life shivering through her again and again.

"Between my legs," she whispered, because she had to know.

She had to know what it would feel like.

On some level she was appalled with herself for failing, yet again, to be as explicit as he'd been. Since when had she become so prudish? She was an academic. Not some sheltered adolescent tucked away in a convent somewhere, unable to form dirty words without imagining she'd be struck down from on high.

But she couldn't seem to make herself say any of the words she might have used. She couldn't seem to force herself to be more specific.

Thor shifted. He bent toward her, and her hips lifted of their own accord, but all he did was press his lips against the inner slope of one thigh.

"Is that what you mean?" he asked, and she could *feel* the words against her tender skin, as if he was tattooing them there with his own lips. As if there was no part of her he wouldn't mark. "I am between your legs, am I not?"

Another wave of heat swept over her. It even pricked at the backs of her eyes, and Margot was suddenly horrified at the notion she might actually cry.

Even more so that she would do it in front of Thor.

Here, while she was supposedly researching Icelandic sex traditions.

She didn't understand how he could be doing these remarkably physical things to her, but her body seemed to want to process them as emotions.

Too many emotions to bear.

Margot didn't *want* to understand.

But she was too hot. She felt raw and exposed, and greedier than she'd ever imagined she could feel. About anything.

It was as if she had never *wanted* before in all her life.

As if everything before this moment was pale. Insubstantial. As pointless as a single candle against the howling blizzard outside.

But she told herself that was the point.

She was here to try to understand this land of fire and ice in the most intimate way possible. The way the locals did.

"My...pussy," she forced herself to say, and managed to get the word out without stuttering like a child. "I want your mouth on my pussy, Thor. Please."

If he noticed that she'd come perilously close to begging after all, he didn't mention it. She felt his mouth curve, there against the soft inside of her thigh. Then he lifted his head and that was worse. Or better.

He looked like some kind of god. Old-world and elemental. Fierce and uncompromising, and entirely bent on destruction.

Margot had never wanted so badly to be destroyed in all her life.

"Your wish is my command," he told her, his voice dark and lazy, with an edge to it that made her wonder a little bit wildly what it would be like to choose to follow his commands.

In the sorts of very specific ways she imagined he practiced nightly in his own, personal dungeon.

He adjusted the way he held her, and she thought he would take the opportunity to make more challenging remarks. To draw this out even further—

But instead he bent and set his mouth there where she needed him the most.

He didn't simply lick into her.

He ate at her.

Thor growled as he feasted on her sodden, tender flesh, then sucked on her clit until she bucked.

He was greedy. Thorough. Impossibly hot. He went back and forth, keeping her on edge and unable to predict what he'd do next—

When the first wave hit her, it seemed to come from nowhere. Margot felt herself stiffen and then the ripples spread, getting more and more intense by the second, until she was jerking against his hold.

And Thor didn't stop.

He rode out her orgasm, as if he wanted to eat it whole, too. And something about that image made it worse—or made it more intense—and so it went on and on and on.

But so did he.

Margot thought she had stopped coming, or maybe it was one long orgasm with no beginning and no end, a rise and a fall and then a lush sweep right back into it all over again.

She went from peak to peak, rolling over and over,

until she lost all awareness of herself. She didn't care if she was too bright, too red. She didn't care that she'd locked her legs around his neck, that she was arched up off the bed in total abandon or that she was grinding her pussy into his mouth.

All she cared about was this. Sensation after sensation, chasing each other toward something bigger. Brighter.

Too wild to name.

Eventually, the storm blew itself out.

Or he decided it had. Margot couldn't tell.

Thor pulled her legs from around him and settled her back on his bed, smiling a little as if he knew exactly how limp and wrung out she was.

Margot couldn't breathe. And the crazy part was, she didn't much care about that the way she knew she had before.

He straightened and stood there over her, and her heart pounded all over again as she stared up at that hard, wicked mouth of his. It was as if he was still pressed against her, his tongue and his teeth and that jaw of his driving her into madness.

How could it be that he didn't even have to do it again? That the memory of what he'd just done pushed her toward that edge all over again…

Margot felt dizzy, but she didn't want to analyze it.

It was easier to look at him instead. So big. So tall. Every inch of him a conquering Viking, packed with hard muscle, that tousled dark blond hair, and those gleaming blue eyes of his that burned wherever they touched her.

And he'd told her to ask for what she wanted, so she did.

"I want your clothes off," she told him, and her heart was still beating too hard, so she couldn't pay attention to how strange she sounded. How unlike herself. "Now."

Thor's mouth didn't move. But she could see the hard sort of smile in the blue of his eyes. He inclined his head and then stretched out his arms to the sides as if he was surrendering.

But she didn't think either one of them believed he was doing anything of the kind.

His eyes were the bluest she'd ever seen. "Do as you like."

It was couched as an invitation. So there was no reason it should have felt like an order.

But there was that fever in her, making it impossible for Margot to care about *feelings*. Not when she was still so wet and greedy.

Not when she still wanted him more than she wanted her next breath.

And the fact that she had never felt that way before—about anyone she'd ever been with or any sex she'd ever thought about having—

Margot couldn't let herself go there.

There were too many precipices littered about and she wanted no part of any of them. Not if considering their danger might make her rethink what she was doing.

She didn't want to rethink it. She didn't want to *think*.

Margot pushed herself up to kneel before him, and a little throbbing thing shook itself awake in a distinct sort of feminine pleasure at the fact he still towered over her.

Something in her shouted that it wasn't right to like this feeling. This strangely compelling sensation that she was small where he was so large, fragile where he was tough, everywhere—

Margot ignored it.

She pushed up the fine, soft T-shirt he wore and worked it over those massive shoulders of his. And her reward was that when she did, his chest was right there before her. His skin was hot to the touch. And he smelled so good it made her eyes water and her belly tighten.

She didn't care if it was right or wrong or what she ought to feel when she followed an urge she didn't recognize and bent forward, pressing her open mouth to the hollow between his pectoral muscles.

But he still wasn't naked and Margot was running out of patience. And nerve. Her fingers felt too big, too clumsy when she wanted to take her time. She wanted to explore every fascinating ridge of his abdomen and all those smooth, heavy muscles that gleamed in the firelight, but there was that dark need deep inside her, winding itself tighter and tighter.

She felt heavy with it. As if she might scream, or cry, or simply burst apart at the seams if she couldn't find her way to that...*more.*

"Why are you frowning?"

Margot hadn't realized she was until he said so. And the amusement in his voice didn't help. She didn't want to tell him that she was desperately trying to keep herself together. That she'd already come too many times and she couldn't seem to stop trembling, down low in her belly. That some part of her was terrified that there was more and that she wanted it so badly.

Or worse, that there wasn't. That she'd already had her fun and Thor would be a disappointment the way she finally admitted to herself many other men had been.

It's unfair to call a mostly satisfying sexual encounter a disappointment, she lectured herself then, the way she always did. *There's no such thing as a sex god. You were there, too.*

But if he'd asked, she would have said that there was no way she could come and come and come again from a little bit of oral sex, either. It wasn't something she'd ever liked all that much, despite how many times her friends—and ex-boyfriends—had told her there must be something wrong with her.

Maybe there wasn't anything wrong with her. Maybe she just hadn't met Thor.

"I want you inside me," she threw at him, and only realized when the words hung between them that she sounded as if she was in the middle of a fight.

Because, of course, he had no idea that she'd just scared herself with her *thoughts*. His blue eyes gleamed too bright, as if he might laugh at her, and that was suddenly the worst thing that she could imagine.

So Margot tilted her chin up and doubled down. "Not your fingers. Not your mouth. Your cock, Thor. Now."

His smile was slow. Languid.

And so hot that Margot felt scalded.

"Yes, Professor," he murmured, as if there was a single part of him that was at all submissive when she could see perfectly well that there was not.

He stepped away and Margot bit her tongue so hard to keep from complaining that it actually hurt. She tasted copper but was happy she'd kept her complaints inside when all he did was move to the side of the bed, rifle through the drawer in his nightstand, then pull out a condom.

Then Thor crawled up onto the great big bed. She hadn't seen him kick off his shoes, but he was barefoot when he threw himself down in the center on his back.

He was also still wearing his trousers.

"Why do you still have clothes on?" she asked, and she could hear the greed and impatience in her voice.

And those other things she refused to acknowledge.

"You didn't take them off," he replied, entirely too much laughter in that voice of his.

Margot scowled at him.

"You should know that the more you do that, the more inviting I find it," he told her, and Margot couldn't tell if he was teasing her.

Or why it made that tight thing inside her seem to flex.

Then hum.

She was no blushing virgin. And yet that was what she felt like with him. Silly, somehow. As if she didn't know herself at all. As if the person who had walked through the doors into this hotel earlier this evening was a complete stranger to this naked creature who was literally panting for a man she'd just met. She wasn't sure she had the slightest idea what to do about that—

But right now she didn't care. She couldn't let herself care.

Margot kept her eyes on Thor's as she crawled toward him. She stopped when she was kneeling beside him, and she wanted—desperately—to conceal the fact that she was breathing so heavily. She could feel her rib cage expand and contract, and worse, she could feel the way her breasts swayed.

But there was no hiding such a thing. She didn't

try, and she told herself that accepting it felt a little bit like power.

When really, the most powerful thing about her at the moment was that molten greediness between her legs. She felt like she was her own furnace.

"Is it your turn to beg?" she asked.

"If you want me to beg, all you need to do is ask me for it." His mouth curved, but it was more a challenge than a smile. "Like anything else on the menu."

Margot didn't have words for the thing she wanted.

Because she wanted everything.

She settled for putting her hands on the waistband of his trousers, still looking at him as she did.

"Are you waiting for me to stop you?" Thor looked almost offensively relaxed for a man who was as hard as he was. Margot could feel the heavy length of his arousal under her hands, leaving her in no doubt that the man was built…proportionally. But he only grinned at her and then folded his arms beneath his head as if he was on a beach somewhere. "Or to give you permission?"

Everything about this—about him—made her bristle.

But it also made her wet.

Wetter.

Margot decided to run with the latter and started to undo his fly. It was slow going because he was so damned hard his cock was pushing up against the fabric, distending the front of his trousers. She ex-

pected him to wince, or hiss out a breath or two, but
not Thor. He stayed where he was, stretched out beneath her like some kind of boneless cat, watching
her with those electric blue eyes of his at half-mast.

And then she didn't care what he was doing because she pulled the great, thick length of him free.
Her mouth actually watered, when she would have
called herself no more interested in performing oral
sex than she was in receiving it. Both could be pleas-
ant, but she believed they got in the way of the good
stuff that she knew how to ride straight to her orgasm.

And yet Margot wanted to lean forward and suck
the thick head of him into her mouth. She wanted
to lick him like a Popsicle until he melted, too. She
hardly knew who the hell she was, practically drool-
ing over the man's cock like this.

But she was a reasonable, rational adult woman
who owned her own sexuality and knew better than
to expect Cirque du Soleil in bed, no matter how glo-
riously sexual and uninhibited Thor had claimed he
was. And she wanted him inside her more than she
wanted to taste him.

Margot told herself that it was giving in to dam-
aging fantasies to imagine that she shouldn't have to
choose between the two when she knew that biology
was biology and masculinity wasn't made of Viagra.

Thor had tossed the condom down beside him
when he'd stretched out on the bed, and she reached
over to swipe it up then. She was aware of him watch-

ing her, but he didn't move. He didn't lift a finger. He didn't even shift his hips when she tugged his trousers down another inch or so to the middle of his thighs.

And somehow that made everything hotter. He let out a breath when she rolled the condom down over his cock, likely because it took a minute to make the edges roll down smoothly over something that big.

"What do you want?" he asked again when the condom was finally in place. And when, to her shame, Margot discovered she was breathing heavily all over again.

"You," she whispered.

"I think you can do better than that."

Later, she promised herself, she would unpack why it was she *wanted* to do better simply because he told her she should. Why she *wanted* to please him. Because all the strange, new things that were tight inside her, winding around and around and making her so shivery, were tied in to that wanting. To her hot, melting pussy, her aching clit and that empty space she wanted him to fill so badly it made her nipples hurt.

"I want…" Her tongue still stung, reminding her that she'd bitten it. And that reminded her that this was research. Fieldwork. An experiment. This wasn't *her*, really. This wasn't who she was or had ever been, and that was probably for the best. "I want to fuck you, Thor."

That wasn't the sort of thing Margot had ever said in bed before, because she'd never been much for talking, much less using dirty, potentially offensive words. She wondered why that was when Thor's blue eyes blazed. His hard mouth curled in one corner and his face seemed to tighten as she watched.

She didn't need him to tell her it was the same greed that throbbed in her, too. She knew.

"Do your worst," he told her, his voice low, dark and with a kick of wildness that seemed connected directly to her—deep inside her.

It felt like the storm outside, battering the windows. Battering her from the inside out.

Margot felt clumsy again, but that didn't stop her. She crawled over him, basking in the heat of him, the clean male scent. She threw her leg over his hips, propped herself up with one hand in the center of his chest, then reached between them to wrap her fingers around the thick head of his cock.

She didn't know what she expected when he shifted beneath her. Directions, maybe. Commentary, almost certainly.

But all Thor did was wrap his hands around her hips, his grip loose and his thumbs resting in the creases of her thighs.

And then did absolutely nothing as slowly, so slowly, Margot began to lower herself onto him.

It was as if everything slowed down with her. As if they were the storm hurling itself against his windows—and somehow every single speck of snow and ice as well.

Margot could feel everything. *Everything.* The way she filled herself with him, inch by thick inch, though she had to pause every other breath to let her body accommodate his size. She could feel the rough fabric of his trousers against her widespread thighs, and the hair that roughened his legs. She was too conscious of her own breath, loud and harsh, but she didn't let it stop her.

She was trembling when she finally took all of him and was flush against him, and she knew he could feel it.

For a moment she could do nothing but sit there, with Thor so deep inside her all she could do was melt and quiver around him. She braced her hands against his abdomen to keep herself upright, but still. It was as if she was caught in that gaze of his. As if she was burning alive.

"This is my favorite handshake," Thor murmured, a kind of inky, addictive darkness in his voice. "This is how you take the measure of a man, is it not?"

"I already know you talk too much."

He smiled at that, but there was something entirely too knowing in his gaze. "Whereas you only talk to hide. But there is no hiding here, Professor."

Margot wanted to object to that. She wanted to defend herself, somehow. Or make him take that back before it lodged inside her the way she could already feel it doing. She wanted to explain herself to him, somehow.

But that could wait.

Because he was stretching her. He filled her, hot and heavy, and that tight thing inside her pulled taut at last.

And she couldn't ignore it. She couldn't pretend it wasn't taking her over like its own kind of desperate fever.

She lifted herself up, then settled down again.

And she could feel that in her toes, her fingertips, her hair—and everything in between.

It wasn't the least bit disappointing, she was forced to notice.

Thor didn't say a word. His thumbs moved idly in that hinge between her thighs and her hips, but he didn't try to take control. He didn't wrap his hands tight around her and slam her down hard against him.

But the fact he could have done those things—that his ability to do it was written all over him and Margot thought she could almost taste it—only made it hotter when he didn't.

And the way he watched her with all that glittering blue male arrogance told her he knew it. Not only did he know it, he was using it against her.

Deliberately.

Because she was the one doing the fucking, but that wasn't what it felt like. She felt as if Thor was hammering into her, holding her down, making her scream and cry and writhe out this mad, red pleasure.

And every time she lifted herself up and slid back

down, it was as if she could feel each and every one of those screams in the back of her throat.

Her breath was harsh and grew harsher. His matched.

Margot went faster and faster.

But it didn't matter how hard she went, how she rocked her hips, how she lost herself in the sweet hitch and the hot slide. There was no getting away from the fact that nothing about this felt appropriately academic.

She felt *alive*. She felt wide-open and exposed. She knew that he could see her—really *see* her—from that flush that rolled over her skin to the way her breasts jiggled as she worked herself against him. She wanted that to distance her from what was happening, what she was doing. She wanted it to throw up a wall.

She wanted something about this to feel the way sex normally felt.

Good, always good, but always *her*.

It wasn't that she didn't feel like herself with Thor, it was that she couldn't tell the difference between them. There was just that brilliant, blistering ache between them, and they were both a part of it.

It was heavy and it was dark. It was bright and it was hot. It was the place where they joined and it was all around them, like the eye of a storm and the driving snow at once, and there was no escaping it.

There was only going toward it.

She felt shattered already, she felt ripped into

pieces and possibly broken, and that was before that crazy fire began to climb to its flashpoint inside her.

Again.

She thought he should have used his fingers. That it should take work, the way it sometimes did, instead of that too-good slide of her clit against him on her lush upstroke.

Margot kept waiting to crash into one of those walls—

But there was nothing there. Just too much sensation, the bluest eyes she'd ever seen and Thor surging inside her over and over again, pounding her out of her own skin and into the ether.

Once. Then again, those hands moving up to grip her waist as she came apart around him.

He held her there, still keeping that same hard pace, making her moans flip over into something that sounded perilously close to screams as he kept going.

And kept going, fucking her straight through that first shattering and into another, far higher and far more dangerous one, because she wasn't entirely sure she'd survive it—

This time he went with her, groaning out something in Icelandic as he pumped himself into her.

And Margot collapsed against that wide, hard chest of his, finally as boneless as he was, tried to catch her breath and waited for the shame of losing herself so completely to claim her.

CHAPTER FOUR

THOR HAD NO idea how long they lay there like that, heaped together on his bed as if neither one of them was likely to walk again under their own power. Or even breathe normally.

He wasn't sure he'd mind.

And it was a sign of how far gone he was that it took a moment for that thought to penetrate the haze he was in like the warning it was.

Margot was sprawled across his chest, her head tucked into the crook of his neck so that all he could see was the bright fall of all that purple. She was breathing deep and low, suggesting that she'd drifted off into sleep.

Or was still lost out there in the storm they'd built together that put the one outside to shame.

And Thor didn't know why he felt...different.

It was more than the simple release of a good orgasm. It felt...layered. Something a little too close to complicated.

As if this woman wasn't like any of the others he'd taken to his bed.

He didn't like anything about it.

He shifted Margot off his body, placing her gently to one side. He meant to jackknife up, head to the bathroom suite and wash the strange, lingering hangover from that truly excellent bit of sex straight off him before the strange layers stuck to him.

But he didn't move.

It took him a minute to realize that he was pressing the palm of one hand against his chest.

He stopped the moment he realized what he was doing. But he found himself frowning, there in his bedroom with the latest winter storm at the window and nothing inside but this confounding, surprising woman and the dance of the fire in its grate.

He felt almost…thrown. And he couldn't have said why, when he was a man very rarely lost for words.

It was something to do with the sheer honesty of Margot's responses. It was the way they'd fit together, the tight grip of her pussy around his cock so good and right it had felt nearly supernatural. It was the way she'd stared down at him as she'd ridden him, those eyes of hers gleaming gold with a kind of wonder in them.

He realized he was quickly becoming maudlin as he lay there. Something he certainly wouldn't have tolerated in anyone else and had no intention of allowing in himself.

Thor rolled to the side of the bed and sat there a moment, amazed that he really did feel as if he'd had too much to drink, even though he had trimmed back on his excesses years before, the better to enjoy all the many things self-control could give him.

He hadn't come close to losing control since. Why did this particular woman test that? When he couldn't recall the last thing that had?

"Are we done?"

Her voice was sleepy. A little bit husky and thick, which lodged itself in Thor's chest as if he was still rubbing his hand there.

He hated that he had to check.

"Do you feel that you collected enough data here? Is your experiment at an end?" Thor wasn't sure he recognized his own voice. He sounded…darker.

Different. Again.

When it was just sex. There was no reason he should feel anything, and certainly not some intangible *difference*. He rubbed his palms over his face to wake himself up from whatever spell this was and ordered himself to get a grip.

"I understand the limitations of male biology, that's all," Margot said.

Thor couldn't quite place that note in her voice, but he knew he didn't like what she was suggesting. He turned his head so he could lift an eyebrow at her over his shoulder.

She'd pulled herself up in the bed. Now she sat

there with the sheet wrapped around her, hugging her own knees.

He would have thought she looked like a child had he not had an instantaneous response to those lush lips of hers that he had felt against his skin, but wasn't allowed to taste.

"I beg your pardon, Professor. What limitations do you imagine I possess?"

Margot's face changed as she gazed back at him, as if she had no idea what her mouth did to him. Her expression was equal parts wistfulness and something a lot more like resignation. "Everybody talks big, Thor. It's part of the game. And I understand it—the urge, anyway."

He found himself perilously close to a scowl and smoothed out his expression, faintly appalled at himself. "You are talking in circles. And I still don't know what you're on about."

"In the heat of the moment I guess it makes everyone feel better to imagine they can go all night long," Margot replied, and even let out a sad little laugh. If Thor was the sort of man who allowed his emotions to get involved with sex, the sound might have pierced him clean through. It was a happy thing indeed that he was not. "This is great as is, really."

"Great?" he echoed.

"Really."

For a moment he assumed she was needling him. Throwing down one of her challenges, because that was who she was—or who she thought she had to be, anyway. But the more he stared at her, there in the center of his bed, the more he was forced to face the disquieting notion that she was being completely sincere.

And it had been a long time since Thor had found himself anything even approaching tongue-tied. After all, he'd made his way in the world on the back of his much-vaunted charm. His ability to talk anyone into anything. It was how he'd managed to build his own little empire at a time when Iceland's economics were shaky at best in the wake of the country's financial collapse.

He didn't really want to think about why it was that this purple-haired American was making him feel like a stranger to himself.

There was that hollow thing in his chest again that he didn't recognize—and more, wanted nothing to do with.

And he had the distinct impression that talking about it would make it a whole lot worse.

Instead, he reached over and took hold of Margot's arm. Then he pulled her toward him across the mattress, until she butted up against him. And the oddness inside him eased a little, because he liked the feel of her skin against his. Maybe too much.

"You could have asked me to come over to the side of the bed," she pointed out, though he could hear the breathlessness in her voice as well as he imagined she could, there in the stillness of the room. "You certainly didn't have to resort to caveman tactics."

"If I was a caveman, I wouldn't have been so gentle."

Margot laughed. Then looked startled, as if she hadn't meant to do that. And it was a different sounding laugh than the one before, as if she'd actually found him funny rather than finding the entire situation disappointing.

But what it meant to Thor was that he had one more item to add to a growing list of things he absolutely shouldn't have been feeling. He made people laugh all the time. It was part of his job, in fact. There was absolutely no reason why this particular laughter should wind its way through him as if he was terribly thirsty and the sound was water.

Why was she getting to him this way?

Thor was doing his own head in.

"Up," he clipped out at her, and when she didn't move fast enough to suit him, he scooped her up in his arms instead.

He stalked across the length of his bedroom while Margot clung to him, her arms going around his neck with an ease that suggested she wasn't as upset by his presumption as her expression suggested.

"Before you complain, a caveman would drag you by your hair, I believe. He would not carry you like this."

She sniffed, but she didn't let go of him. "I think

you can agree that there is an inherent gender disparity in—"

"If you would like to pick me up, high against your chest, and then cart me across a room, Margot," he said silkily, "you are welcome to do so at any time."

Her face was so close to his like this, and he found his gaze drawn back to her lips. That mouth of hers that fascinated him far more than was likely healthy.

Thor had never thought too much about kissing. It was a part of things, yes. It was always on the menu. But he'd never been alive with the need to put his mouth on someone else's. He'd never found himself daydreaming about how another person might taste. He'd never thought the fact that he was forbidden to kiss a woman might very well kill him.

Until now.

"The world would be a very different place if I could do that," Margot said quietly, and he had the impression she'd spent longer than the last few seconds thinking about what it would be like to have a man's strength. "History would have taken a very different path."

"Perhaps." Thor walked them both into his bathroom, which featured a walk-in shower with a variety of showerheads, perfect for a very large man and any situation he might find himself in. He had endeavored not to think too closely about why his birth father, a known *libertine* of the first order, might have required such a space. "But would you truly wish to live in that world?"

"Yes."

"You seem so sure."

"I've been pretty sure about equality and how I want it since I could spell it. And I taught myself how to read, and spell, really young."

"Equality is a worthy goal, certainly. But that comes from inside. That is how we think. How we raise our children and what we demand of our leaders and fellow citizens, yes? It is in many ways an intellectual exercise. What we do with these bodies, that will never be the same no matter what we think—that is something else."

He set her down just inside the glass doors of the shower and smiled when the frown he expected to see on her face was right there, as anticipated. But the floors in the bathroom were heated the same way everything was in Iceland, with all that geothermal goodness, and Margot sighed a little as her feet hit the tiles as if she'd expected to find them cold and unpleasant. And as if she was almost shocked when they weren't.

That felt a bit too much like the sort of metaphor he had absolutely no desire to think about too closely, because sex wasn't about metaphors. It was about sex—or he was doing it wrong.

Thor reached in and fiddled with the water until it was pouring down from all directions and steam billowed up. And he shoved *metaphors* out of his head, then told himself he wasn't the least bit uneasy, or layered, or any of those other things he didn't want to feel.

Just because this woman felt different, it didn't mean *he* had to act any differently than he normally would.

He stepped inside the shower as well, nudging her to go farther when she hung back from the actual fall of the hot water.

"You look as if you might jump out of your skin at any moment," he observed.

Next to him, Margot smiled, though it looked awkward. She slicked her hair back with both hands, making it look much darker with the wet and steam in it. And it was impossible, really, to notice anything on her face at all save her huge dark gold eyes. And that damned mouth.

Maybe, Thor thought then, he was the one who was damned.

"I'm not used to all this…naked time," she said after a moment.

Thor ordered himself to stop staring at her mouth like a crazed person. To try to summon up some of that charm of his he'd been so sure of down in the bar. "You don't get naked?"

"I get naked alone, yes. And I shower alone. I also dress myself alone, before you ask. I'm not sure how I feel about making it a communal activity."

"But we are all of us just bodies," Thor said.

"Flesh and blood. Bones and sinew. Beautiful in our own ways."

And there was something about the heat, the wet. It sank into him, smoothing out the edges of that hollow place in his chest. Or maybe it was her. His suspicious professor. Maybe it was something about the way Margot tipped her head back to look up at him, and didn't seem to care that her mouth looked so vulnerable.

He had the disarming notion that it was entirely too possible that she didn't know.

"Of course," she said, but her voice had gone soft. Ragged. "Just bodies. Just a selection of interlocking parts. Nothing but a complicated handshake or two, the way people like to perform them."

Thor wasn't thinking. That was what he told himself, anyway. The water pounded down around them, locking them away in all the steam and heat. He reached over and found her hand, one and then the next. He laced their fingers together into a new kind of complicated handshake and then backed her up until she was pressed against the slickness of the far wall.

Her lips parted a little, just enough to drive him crazy. Vulnerable and challenging at once, and he… forgot himself. He bent his head and moved to fit his mouth to hers—

"No," she said, though the word sounded like more of a question. "No kissing, remember?"

Thor didn't want to remember. He wanted to taste her. He wanted to glut himself on her.

He *wanted* in ways as new to him as she was.

But he acquiesced, dropping his head to the line of her neck instead. And his hands rose almost of their own accord, lifting hers until he could pin them, one on either side of her head—and that mouth she continued to deny him.

"Thor…" she moaned as he made her shiver.

It was only sex. They were only bodies.

Or so he kept telling himself.

He didn't want to feel hollow. He didn't want to feel anything at all except sated. He dropped to his knees before her, finding her nipples again. He let go of one of her hands and traced his way down the length of her body as he sucked on one breast, exulting in the broken little moans she let out.

He found her pussy wet. Hot. And he didn't wait. He plunged his fingers deep inside her, using his thumb to drag against her clit on the outstroke.

Thor didn't know what he was proving. He didn't know what he was trying to do.

But then he didn't care, because Margot was so ripe and so lush and she came apart beneath his hands and his mouth as if she had been put on this earth for that purpose alone.

Just bodies, he told himself as Margot's cries echoed off the tiles of his shower.

Thor told himself that was what he had wanted. Exactly that sound she made. The way she clenched around his fingers. The sweet velvet of her nipples, the way she threw her head back, the line of her throat as she gave herself over to abandon.

That was what he wanted. Nothing else.

Because there was nothing else, he told himself sharply, no matter how beautifully she came for him.

He stood and didn't know what he meant to do next. There were too many competing things fighting for supremacy inside him. Too many of those layers he didn't want to admit were there.

It took a moment for Margot's eyes to open, but when they did, they were bright gold.

And she smiled—and this time there was nothing the least bit awkward about it. It felt a little too much like spring to a man who'd been raised in relentless winter.

She didn't say a word. She simply knelt down before him and tipped her head back so he could see the exquisite hunger all over her face. She wrapped her hands around his cock, smiled again and took him deep into her mouth.

"Look at you," Margot murmured after she'd sucked him in deep and then taken her time dragging her mouth off him again, scraping her teeth against the back of his head as she went. "You really do defy your own biology, don't you?"

But she didn't give him a chance to answer. And Thor couldn't think straight when she took him deep in that mouth of hers again and again.

Her mouth was so hot. Her tongue moved against

the plump head of his cock, swirling and dancing and sending that crackling electric current all throughout his body. He leaned back against the wall of the shower, slightly concerned his legs might give out, and anchored himself with one hand sunk deep in her streaming wet hair.

But he didn't try to guide her. He wanted to see what she'd do, so he let her do her worst.

And Margot explored him. She licked him up and down as if he was dessert, and then she took him in deep, as if she was teaching herself how to deep throat right here in his own shower.

He meant to pull out. To give her warning or lift her up against him so he could ride her into completion again—but she didn't stop. It was as if she felt his balls tighten, his whole body stiffen, and she took him in even deeper—

Then listened to him groan as he poured himself down her throat.

And when he pulled himself out of her mouth at last, she was still kneeling there, her face tipped up to his while the water fell all around her, her smile wide and pleased.

Something gleaming brighter than gold in her gaze.

And Thor knew this was more than a run-of-the-mill hangover.

His professor was trouble.

CHAPTER FIVE

"You must be hungry," Thor said with a kind of easy courtesy that reminded her who he was. What he did.

And why she was here.

Margot was grateful. She was humming inside, as if she'd been tuned to a station she couldn't hear with her ears but could feel in every part of her flesh and deep into her bones. She didn't know what was happening to her, but that humming thing made it impossible to find that as terrifying as she might have otherwise. As perhaps she should have.

There was some kind of magic in this place, she couldn't keep herself from thinking, and it didn't seem to matter that she was a rational woman of scientific inquiry who didn't believe in magic.

There was some kind of magic in this man, too.

It wasn't that Margot had ever disliked performing oral sex, per se, because she didn't. She hadn't. It wasn't her favorite thing in the world to do, of course, but it was always the other aspects of the act that had gotten to her more than the main event.

Like the positions it required her to get into. Kneeling, for example. So submissive and problematic, especially when a man wrapped his hands in her hair as if he wanted to control her head—and then often did.

Yet doing it to Thor had been a completely new and different thing. She hadn't suffered through it without getting much out of it herself because that was what grown adults sometimes did in service to their partners' needs, the way she always had in the past.

She'd loved every second of it.

Margot was going to need to interrogate herself at length about the things this man made her feel, all those twisted things she'd thought she'd evolved past years ago, but she still felt slippery. Her pussy felt swollen into a kind of shivery ripeness. Her skin was overly sensitive, all over, so that every brush of the soft, cashmere wrap Thor had settled around her sent spirals of pleasure all through her.

He had washed her. He'd used those big hands, if not in the dark ways she'd wanted, and the soap he'd made into a thick lather between his palms. Something about the attention he'd paid to every square inch of her body had tugged at her, but Margot hadn't wanted to say anything to break the spell. She couldn't say she'd enjoyed that fierce look of concentration on his face so much as she'd thrilled to it.

It had made her feel whole and even cherished in ways she didn't know how to process.

And there was something wrong with her. Something terribly wrong, down into her wiring. She understood it, but she couldn't seem to bring herself to analyze it the way she knew she should. But her *wrongness* glowed there, deep in her gut and splashed all over her skin.

What bothered her was that she didn't care about that, here with Thor, as much as she should have.

For one thing, she'd liked it far too much when she'd been on her knees in that shower, Thor's cock in her mouth. She'd wished that Thor had used that hand of his in all the dark, dirty ways she would have hated if anyone else had tried. She'd wanted to feel what it was like to be under his control, no matter how problematic.

He hadn't done anything with the hand in her hair except hold it there, and Margot had found herself entertaining wild fantasies, what-ifs… What if he held her head where he wanted it? What if he controlled the pace, the depth of each thrust?

What if he…took her over completely?

Her pussy ached even imagining it.

And she knew she ought to be ashamed of the way she melted more and more at each dark and dirty little *what-if* that she could come up with.

Letting him wash her had been much the same. *This is the ultimate objectification*, her brain had argued, but the rest of her hadn't cared. He'd tended to her as if she was his possession. Something precious to him, something he needed and cared for.

Something he owns, a voice in her had supplied.

And she knew that she should have been sickened by the very idea.

But instead, she had felt soothed. Adored, even. Thor had washed her everywhere. He'd even washed her hair. His hands were so big and she knew all the things they could do to her body, but there in the shower he had gently, carefully washed her clean as if doing so was his responsibility. His privilege.

And when they'd gotten out, he'd bundled her in a huge towel and dried her off as if that, too, was a part of this ritual he needed to perform. And despite all the words that crowded into her head—*infantilizing, condescending, daddy issues, problematic*—Margot had stood there and basked in his attention.

And that humming in her had continued.

Now she sat with her legs crossed on the low-slung couch to one side of the fireplace in his bedroom that should have been too big to feel cozy but somehow managed it despite its unwieldy size. He had exchanged the big, fluffy bath towel for this almost unbearably warm and soft wrap she wore now, and Margot told herself that she was merely drying her hair by the fire. That there was nothing to it but that.

That she wasn't watching Thor as he moved around the room. That she wasn't marveling in the things firelight did for a man as sculpted as he was.

He was all muscle and sinew, cast in liquid gold thanks to the crackling flames.

"Are you in a trance?" he asked, and she realized with a jolt that he had been standing there, waiting for her response, for some time.

Margot cleared her throat. "Yes," she said, striving for that same overtly polite tone, the sort she'd have used if a waiter had caught her daydreaming in a fancy restaurant. "I think I'm starving, actually."

"I will send down to the kitchen for some food." She didn't know when he'd pulled on those athletic trousers he wore now, but they rode low on his hips, making it impossible for her to do anything but marvel at that ridge shaped like a V that pointed down beneath his waistband.

"Why are you taking care of me?" Margot asked.

And then wished she hadn't.

Thor's gaze found hers, something like affront in all that blue. He held up a finger, then spoke into the phone at his ear. Margot caught only the odd word here and there as he spoke in rapid Icelandic, never dropping her gaze.

When the call was finished, he dropped the hand holding the phone to his side as he regarded her for another long moment that seemed to scrape through her.

Maybe that was why she kept talking, when every word that spilled over her tongue made her feel more exposed. "I just mean that none of this is necessary.

You're treating me like some kind of treasured guest when I'm not. It's supposed to be an experiment—"

"Yes, yes. Only an experiment. So you keep telling me. I was unaware that meant I should fuck you and then throw you out in the hall like rubbish."

There was an edge to his voice that Margot didn't understand. But she didn't particularly want to acknowledge it, either.

"I want to make sure that we're not blurring any boundaries here, that's all," she said coolly, and hoped that he couldn't see that she was blurry all the way through. So blurry she could hardly see straight.

That edge in his voice seemed locked on his mouth then. "Because I wish to eat? Because sex can work up an appetite? These are hard boundaries of yours that cannot be crossed?"

"You said yourself that Icelanders prefer sex to dinner dates."

"Think of it as fuel." His blue eyes glittered. She had the strangest notion that she had offended him, somehow. "After all, the blizzard rages on. And inside, it is warm and safe and the night is young."

"You can't possibly…" She drifted off, her gaze following that tempting V all the way down.

Where, if she wasn't mistaken, his cock was stirring yet again.

"How old are you?" she asked in disbelief.

And whatever tension had been building there between them, it shattered when he laughed. That same mighty laugh that reminded her where she was, tucked up here on the top of the world in this land of trolls and dark and men who were named for very old gods, she wondered if she could see in his face.

"Are you worried that I'm an adolescent boy?" he asked. "I regret to inform you that I haven't been anything like an adolescent in a very long while."

"If you say so."

"Adolescent boys have erections as easily as breathing, it is true." Thor was still laughing, and it was unfair, the things that did to his already too-beautiful face. "But it is like a summer storm. All that noise and carrying on, yet they do not have any control."

"But you do."

Another laugh, and it was just as dangerous as before. "Do you doubt it? I'm sorry. I must have lost track of how many times I made you come."

She felt her ears get hot. Some part of her wanted to curl into a ball and hide under the couch, but he'd told her about this. Icelanders talked about sex. With a frankness that made every last bit of Margot's Midwestern soul curl up and want to die.

But she told herself this, too, was part of the experiment she was conducting.

She inclined her head. "I counted."

His smile was delighted. And infinitely wicked. "I am pleased to hear that. I did, too."

"I suppose it could be the novelty," she continued, frowning a little. "As you said yourself, there's no such thing as a sex god. There's chemistry. But that always wears off, usually pretty quickly."

"Here is what I do not understand." Thor moved to sit down, and he didn't choose the chair across from the couch like a civilized person might have while discussing this research project they were undertaking together. Instead, he settled himself on the other end of the same couch where she sat, making it that much smaller in an instant. And he did it in that same languid, boneless way he did everything, lounging there and taking up more than his fair share of the couch, which only made Margot frown. "Your field of study is sex, is it not?"

Her frown deepened. "Well, sex is a fairly broad category, obviously, and my specialty is significantly narrower because I'm primarily concerned with—"

"I will take that as a yes."

"—human sexuality in cultural contexts. I'm specifically intrigued by the particular intersection—"

"Professor. Control yourself." And there was that curve in his mouth again, which meant that when she obeyed him it felt like some kind of caress. She didn't understand that, either, but it made that humming thing inside her grow deeper. Louder. "I don't want to debate your thesis. I'm sure it's fascinating. What specifically intrigues me is that you live and breathe sex in your work, yet seem singularly disposed to take the joy out of it. Why is that?"

"I don't think I do that at all."

"I have known you for a few hours and already I understand that you think sex is in many ways a chore, that you think chemistry comes and goes and cannot be depended upon. You think men cannot control their penises and you have a great many strange ideas about what any man is capable of in the course of an evening. You seemed astounded that I made you come at all, much less over and over again."

Margot felt as if she'd fallen, hard, knocking all the air out of her body. "I think you've read me wrong."

He lifted his shoulder, then dropped it, and even as she struggled for breath, it was impossible not to notice how beautiful he was and, worse than that, how she could *feel* him in parts of her body that she'd never paid all that much attention to before.

"Who have you been sleeping with?" he asked in that same mild tone.

And ordinarily, of course, Margot would have been outraged at a question like that. A person's sexual history was no one else's business, unless she chose to share it of her own volition. But something about the way Thor had asked the question kept her from reacting like that.

His tone was so...cool. His gaze was clinical.

It was exactly what she should have wanted. She couldn't understand why she didn't like it much.

"I never pick men up in bars while drunk, if that's what you mean," she heard herself say. "Not that I'm suggesting that there's anything wrong with that. I support sex positivity in all its forms. Everyone should be able to enjoy sex wherever they find it, in whatever way they like it, as long as it doesn't harm anyone and assuming they're able to voice their explicit consent."

"Everyone should be able to do these things, yes. Of course. But you do not."

She didn't. She'd never really enjoyed sex that way, with the kind of cheerful merriment that she thought she should have, but Margot didn't know why it made her uncomfortable to say so. Out loud, anyway.

To Thor, who had made her come over and over and over with what even she had to admit had seemed a lot like reckless abandon.

"I've had partners, Thor. I just met them under different circumstances."

"How mysterious. Did you grow them in a lab somewhere?"

"In a manner of speaking, yes. I spend most of my time on university campuses, after all. I've met most of the partners I've had through academics in one way or another."

"I see. You are usually seized with a sudden passion while flipping through piles of research books, or some such thing."

She frowned. "Not quite. I'm not sure I've ever been seized by passion, thank you. That sounds like something that ought to be checked out by a medical health professional." Thor laughed, and Margot kept going. "I meet a man. We talk. We usually talk quite a lot, in fact. How else can you possibly know if you suit?"

Thor's mouth curved. "You fuck them, Margot. You can talk until you're blue in the face. You can tell each other all manner of stories. You can compliment each other on your smart ideas and funny jokes. But if you have no sexual chemistry, then all you can ever truly be is friends."

"Not everything is about sex."

"Perhaps not. But I think you'll find that fucking usually is."

"You're obviously looking for a more physical sort of relationship than I am. I couldn't possibly consider someone as a partner if I didn't feel that we connected on an intellectual level, and I'd always choose a very good friend with an astonishing brain over a fuck or two."

"Why must you make that choice?"

She smiled at him. "You and I are different people. We look for different things."

"I can't decide if that was sad or patronizing."

"I'm not trying to insult you. You don't have to understand the things I need. I'm a tenured professor. You—"

She stopped herself, but it was too late. His dark blond brows lifted.

"I own a sex hotel and can therefore be assumed to have no intellectual interests whatsoever. A great and glorious *tenured professor* such as you, of course, is such a towering mind that you could never find yourself enslaved by the demands of the flesh." But he laughed. "Am I your intellectual equal, Professor? Because I suspect your body likes me just fine."

"It doesn't matter who likes what here. You're not my partner."

"Indeed I am not." That sat there between them. Margot told herself it was absurd that her pulse should racket about like that while he regarded her, all narrowed blue gaze and that humming thing inside her. "But you still haven't answered the question. Why do you study sex if you think it is little more than a physical expression of what sounds to an impartial observer like a series of very long, very boring conversations?"

"Some people are more captivated by the mind than the body."

"You are not one of those people." He shook his head when Margot scowled at him. "What fascinates me is why you think otherwise. Because you have a job that involves your mind? So do many others. Why do you seem to think that your body and your mind aren't connected? You can't have one without the other."

Margot drew the wrap tighter around her. "I think you're misunderstanding me."

"Proving, yet again, that I am not your intellectual equal, yes? Or is it that no one can be your intellectual equal? That must be convenient."

Margot's eyes narrowed. "I don't think I asked you to psychoanalyze me."

"I'm merely offering up my humble observations. It is my contribution to science, nothing more. After all, this is an experiment, is it not?"

And now there was a kind of prickly thing deep inside Margot that she didn't understand. She should have no interest at all in explaining herself to this man. She never had to see him again after the blizzard ended. In fact, she could demand that he give her that hotel key right now and let her go off to a room somewhere. She didn't have to tolerate any of this.

And yet there was something in her that wanted—needed—to explain.

The worst part was the little voice whispering that the need came from the same place as the part of her that had loved kneeling down before him. The part of her that had drifted off into the kinds of fantasies she normally strictly forbade herself to have, because they were remnants of patriarchal harm that every woman carried around inside her. They weren't real. She'd never allowed herself to believe they could possibly be real.

She should have forbidden herself this, too. And yet here she was, opening up her mouth.

"Sex is fascinating," she told him as if her life depended on it. As if she was on trial. "Why wouldn't I want to study it? You've built your life around sex, too, as far as I can tell."

"I built my life around pleasure. I'm not sure it's the same thing."

"What interests me are the ways that sexuality fuels change. If it does." She thought about the things she'd wanted him to do in that shower. The way she'd wanted to exult in his strength, his control. "What it means if it does. Can a philosophical need translate into a sexual one?"

"That sounds as if you think we are all able to pick and choose our sexualities."

"I don't think that." She shifted against the couch. "But I do think that we have a responsibility to make certain our expression of our sexualities doesn't betray our principles."

Thor sighed and ran one of his big hands through his hair. "You either think something is hot or you don't, Professor. It either gets you off or it doesn't. The end."

"I don't think it's that simple."

"Which is why you have created this life of yours that celebrates all the many ways you have complicated basic needs."

"Because you know best, of course. I can't possibly know myself or what I actually find hot. It can't be that people are different and want different things."

"I don't know about people in general," Thor said with that mildness that the heat in his gaze completely contradicted, and it made her stomach twist, then drop. "But I do know about you. Or maybe you've forgotten already."

"I had a few orgasms, yes," Margot threw back at him, and forced herself to unclench her teeth. "Forgive me if I don't think that makes you a god."

"I am not the one who considers myself a sex god. Nor am I the one who found each successive orgasm quite so overwhelming. This leads me to imagine that you are not so used to coming and coming and then coming again. And that, Professor, suggests that the kind of sex you are used to having is perhaps a little too intellectual."

"There's no such thing as *too* intellectual," she gritted out.

"If you say so."

"There's nothing wrong with intellect. Thinking is not a bad thing."

He didn't laugh, but she could see the gleam of it in his blue gaze. "I don't believe I said it was."

"I'm not embarrassed by the fact I'm more intellectual than physical. I like it that way."

Thor smiled. "And yet you are the one who appears upset. You are the one who feels there must be a separation between your head and your body."

Margot realized she was clenching her fists in frustration and forced herself to straighten out her fingers before she tore the airy cashmere draped around her.

"My father was an academic, too," she said after a moment, and she had no idea where that had come from. She never talked about her family. But tonight had been filled with things she never did. "He's a remarkably intelligent man who could spend days playing chess and conducting rousing debates. I was raised to prize that kind of intellectual engagement above all things. And I discovered as I grew that I agreed with the way I was raised. That I want the same things."

"Chess and a rousing debate."

"Yes." She lifted her chin. "I like people who arrange their lives around ideas."

"Let me guess. The only way your father gave you any kind of attention was if you proved your intellect to him."

Too late Margot realized her mistake. She didn't want to talk about her father like this. Or at all. She didn't want to tear apart her family's dynamics and expose them here in this powerfully strange place. She didn't want to talk about what it had been like to be raised the only child of towering intellect and swaggering academic genius Ronald Cavendish. She didn't want to recount the number of times she had fallen short of her father's expectations, confronted over and over again with her own limitations. Or the many ways she still did.

And she definitely didn't want to talk about her mother. Or all the ways Margot had learned since her earliest days that a marriage that wasn't between intellectual equals was like a stifling prison at best and something far grimmer than that at worst. She'd seen it with her own eyes. She'd lived it.

So instead she frowned at the door as if she could make their food come quicker that way. And so she didn't have to watch the way Thor was studying her and likely seeing far too much.

"Fathers are tricky," she said. "Take yours, while we're on the subject." He went very still at that, there beside her, but he didn't protest. So she forged on ahead. "Your last name, for example. Shouldn't it be Danielsson rather than Ragnarsson? Your actual father's name was Daniel St. George."

"Thank you. I am aware of Iceland's patronymic conventions." He sighed, but she'd been looking at the door. By the time she turned to him, he was only gazing back at her in that mild way that made her wonder how he got anyone to believe he wasn't wildly dangerous when it was that very studied languidness that announced it. "My mother married my stepfather before she had me, and when she did, they both decided to give me his name because my mother never expected to see my father again. And indeed, she did not."

It was as if being around this man had opened up dark pockets inside her that she had never known were there. Because she felt something like envy at his flippant, careless tone. The things he said should have been upsetting, surely. But Thor didn't look upset in the least. He merely lounged there, as if there was no story at all to how he came to be raised as another man's son.

Meanwhile, Margot couldn't say anything bad had ever happened to her outside of her father's disappointment in her. She hadn't been treated badly. Her needs had always been met. Her parents had supported her academic aspirations all the way. So why wasn't she relaxed and flippant in turn?

"I'm no tremendous intellect, but even a dullard like me recognizes an attempt to change the subject when it appears before him," Thor said quietly.

"I do not have daddy issues," Margot snapped.

"Then you would be remarkable indeed." His blue gaze was kind, and Margot found that unacceptable because it made her want to cry. "Are we not all stitched together by our pasts? And is the thread not often the color of the people who raised us?"

Margot could feel her heartbeat, each thud like a nail into a coffin. *Her* coffin, she had no doubt.

"I don't want to talk about needlework," she threw at him. "I don't want to talk at all. You told me Icelanders communicate with sex, not idle chitchat."

"I would not call something that makes you this upset *idle*, Professor."

"I'm not upset." When the elevator sounded from

the main room, announcing the arrival of their food, she was almost pathetically grateful. She forced herself to smile. "But maybe I'm a little bit hungry."

Thor took his time getting to his feet. He kept his gaze on her, and Margot would have given anything to look away. To hide. To pull on her clothes and run.

But she couldn't seem to move.

"Very well," he said after a moment, when he was standing there before her again. "I look forward to all the epic, athletic, silent sex we'll be having once you replenish your energy stores and restore your delightful mood."

"That's why we're here, isn't it? I'm tired of all this talking."

Because she couldn't seem to help herself. And because anything was better than the unwieldy things sloshing around inside her, threatening to tip over and poison her there and then.

His smile was like a weapon. "I'll endeavor not to hold myself back any longer, then, shall I?"

Thor left her there as he walked toward the elevator, her heart like a lump in her throat and her body alive with a new sort of fire, wondering what fresh hell she'd dropped herself in this time.

And why she couldn't seem to do anything but stay right where she was.

Shivering with anticipation.

CHAPTER SIX

It took about three seconds for the silence to get to Margot. They both sat back from the meal having eaten their fill in a way that felt a bit too much like fueling for an ultramarathon.

Or perhaps it was less the silence and more the way Thor was looking at her from the other side of the table as he lounged there. It made her skin feel too tight. It made her entirely too aware of the way she was—or wasn't—breathing.

"I think this is a perfect opportunity to take a moment to reflect and reassess," Margot began in her best professor's voice, as if pretending she was delivering a lecture could help her feel a little safer in her own skin.

"This is a time for silence, Margot," Thor replied, cutting her off, his voice low and dark. Or not dark, exactly. It was astounding how much he seemed a part of the blustery night outside that made the windows shudder. "No more talking. Isn't that what you requested?"

She might have. She wasn't sure she could remember her own name when he looked at her like that, much less what she might have said earlier.

Thor stood without another word and came around the table. He took her hand and lifted her to her feet there before him. And Margot let him. She more than let him. She went as easily as if these were steps to a dance they'd choreographed and practiced a thousand times before.

"I can't promise I won't say something." Margot didn't mind that she sounded defiant. But it was the shakiness in her voice that she was afraid might haunt her forever.

"You won't."

Thor reached down and plucked something from the table. It took her a moment to understand what it was. An untouched snow-white cloth napkin.

And it took her still another moment to understand why Thor was offering it to her.

Something slammed through her, dark and mad.

"You can't be serious. You're not going to put..." Margot's words deserted her, especially when she saw all the *intent* in his gaze and the patience he wielded the way other men used their fists. "Why am I not surprised that you want to gag a woman?"

If she'd expected him to be offended at that, she was disappointed. His eyes gleamed as if she'd told a good joke.

"Women routinely beg me to gag them," Thor

murmured. "Among a great many other things I suspect you would pretend to find appalling."

"I'm not sure I'd be pretending."

That blue gleam intensified. "Do women whose desires differ from yours deserve to have them met?"

Margot scowled at him. "Of course."

"I ask because I get the distinct impression that you use your academic reflections to judge these things."

"Academic reflection is a conversation, not a condemnation."

"What I think is that you hide in these words of yours. These ideas you have decided are true without having experienced them yourself. Meanwhile, you have no idea what your body wants because you talk yourself out of it." Thor ran a finger down her cheek as if he found her scowl delightful, and smiled when goose bumps prickled to life across her shoulders at the light touch. "What I am offering you is a chance to explore that directly. What if you can't speak? What would happen then?"

"I would be handing over my voice to a man, the way women have done for millennia. Why would that be appealing?"

"But this is not 'millennia.' This is here, now. Tonight. I am one man, not the whole of the patriarchy arrayed against you. And I don't want to take your voice from you, Margot. I want to hear what other things you have to say when you can't rely on your mouth."

She stared at him for what felt like nine or ten millennia, if not more, but Thor only gazed back at her as if he could wait forever.

And somehow that let her ignore all the shrieking things in her head and focus on the places where she melted and ached for him. She thought about the dark fantasies she didn't dare speak out loud and would have denied she had, if asked. The things she'd never told another living soul and hardly admitted to herself.

What he was offering was a chance to explore them. And if she couldn't talk, she couldn't talk herself out of it, could she?

"There has to be a signal," she said, still scowling at him. "I have to be able to tell you to stop if I want you to stop."

"There is a very simple signal. All you have to do is remove the gag. Then say whatever it is you wish to say. Tell me to stop. Tell me to never stop. Tell me whatever you like—but understand that the goal is to see if you can tell me all the things that go on in that beautiful head of yours without uttering a single word."

There was a different sort of tremor making its way through her then. Margot shook, but on the inside. Her eyes felt too glassy, and she worried that all the uncertain, off-center things tilting and slopping around inside her were close to spilling over and revealing her.

You've already revealed yourself, a stern voice in her head chimed in then. *Repeatedly.*

But Margot knew, somehow, that there was so much more.

And she was worried about the things he might do to her. She was worried she might hate them— but if she was honest, she was far more concerned that she might not hate them at all.

And, most of all, she was worried that if she didn't do it, if she didn't take this opportunity no matter how it made her shake inside, no matter what it said about her or what it made her to even entertain the notion, she would regret it for the rest of her life.

It sat there between them, as stark and unrelenting as the coldly masculine room they stood in. As Thor himself, waiting there before her. As irrevocable as that pounding, swirling storm that beat at the windows and sounded too much like her terrified, deliriously wanton heart.

She didn't want to do this. She only knew she had to, or die.

And it didn't matter how many times Margot told herself she was being needlessly melodramatic. The feeling she had to do this—*she had to*—only grew the longer she stood there.

"What do you get out of it?" She hadn't meant to ask that question, but once she had, she found she desperately wanted to know the answer. It was her turn to study Thor for a moment, and she found herself lingering on the sharp blades of his cheekbones as if they were clues. "What do you like about playing games like this?"

"Other than the sex?"

But she didn't believe the lazy way he said that, as if all he cared about was getting his end away.

"This isn't about sex. Or not only sex. If it was, you wouldn't be quite so concerned with how I use my voice or what words I choose."

"I don't know that I would consider sex a game at all. Intimacy is not a few sets of tennis on a summer afternoon, is it?"

Margot was tempted to comment on the game of tennis itself, and more specifically its scoring system that used *love* to mean *zero*, but refrained. She had a feeling that what sounded clever in her head would sound very different here in this cavernous room with her very own Viking.

"If you play at it, is it really intimacy at all?" she asked instead.

"I am not certain that I am the one playing," Thor said. He didn't back away as he spoke. He stayed right where he was, big and tall and taking up entirely too much space without seeming to try very hard. Or notice it. "You are the one who needs a university-sanctioned research project to allow yourself to push your own boundaries. I do not require these masks and charades. If I want to fuck, I fuck. The end."

It was something she knew firsthand now, though Margot found she still couldn't quite believe it. Not quite. No matter that she was close enough to naked and could still feel him all over her, like a new tattoo.

"But sometimes you do it with gags. And whips and chains or other such implements in a dungeon built for precisely that sort of transgressive sex, presumably."

"You seem unduly concerned with a dungeon you have never seen." Thor laughed, a low, rolling scrape of sound that made her feel entirely too warm. "If you would like to experience it, Professor, you need only ask. Here in this hotel we exist to satisfy your every desire."

She ignored that last part and concentrated on the issue at hand. The issue that was literally still *in* his hand. "I don't think it's unreasonable to assume that playing sex games with gags operates as a training ground for the kinds of things people decide they need to do in dungeons."

"Not everything I do has an agenda." Thor laughed again, though this time it felt more like fire. "I am not a vaunted professor of human sexuality, after all. I am merely a lowly practitioner of the art."

Margot found herself smiling the way she did at unruly first-year students. "You and I both know what kind of power dynamic a gag indicates. Don't

insult my intelligence by pretending that could be
an accident on your part. What I'm wondering now
is if that's part of who you are. Were you a sexual
dominant before you came into possession of a sex
hotel? Or is that something working here brought out
in you? And how does sexual dominance work in a
country filled with women so passionately feminist?
Does that complicate it?"

Thor's laugh was louder than before, and this time
when he reached out to move his fingers over her
cheek, Margot could have sworn there was something affectionate in the way he did it. And in the
way he gazed at her.

But she couldn't allow herself to dwell on that.
This was about work, not her lonely little heart.

She was instantly horrified that she was thinking about her heart at all. Much less in those terms.

"I try not to complicate my sexual desires unnec-
essarily," he said drily. "And I'm not sure that I think
the practice of sexual dominance and feminism are at
odds anywhere but in the heads of skeptics who are
more concerned with metaphors than with scream-
ing, delirious orgasms."

"There is not a single submissive bone in my
body," Margot gritted out.

And only realized once she did that he hadn't argued otherwise.

The curve in his mouth felt like an indictment.
"If you say so."

"You know what strikes me as notably un-feminist? You believing you know what I want better than I do."

He was still so close, and that meant she could see the way his blue eyes gleamed. It made every hair on the back of her neck prickle, the way the dance of the northern lights across these far northern skies did. As if he was that elemental and otherworldly.

She told herself he was just a man. Nothing more and nothing less.

No matter that there was a part of her that wanted to make him a myth instead.

"What I believe is that all of us are made of a storm of competing desires and needs," Thor said, almost gently. As if he knew the real storm was the one happening inside Margot. "Some of us privilege one over the other. Some of us take pride in our labels, but these are always attempts to control the uncontrollable, are they not? You are the expert, after all. Surely you must know this already. People can talk. People can define themselves and others in any number of ways. But desire, passion, need—these things are not quantifiable no matter how we might wish they were. And for all our advances across the centuries, no one has yet figured out how to control them."

"I don't believe in that kind of passion," Margot whispered.

She didn't. She knew she didn't and she never had. She had written papers on the subject of passion and the many ways people tried to personify the feeling. Because if it was a kind of person, a being, they could blame it for all manner of things, like a demon of yore. A devil intent on their destruction.

If passion was responsible, the actual person in question need never be.

But there was something about saying it out loud, here, to Thor, that made her gut tighten as if she'd told him a lie.

"Passion is like truth, I am afraid," Thor told her, almost sorrowfully. "It does not require your belief to exist."

"You haven't answered the question."

He lifted the hand that held that bright white napkin, but the way he waved it between them had nothing to do with surrender. Or, at least, not his surrender. "And you have gone to great lengths to avoid this little bit of cloth, have you not?"

Margot's heart gave a terrific thump in her chest, or maybe it was in her belly. Or her pussy, where she felt a sharp jolt. It was everywhere. It was all of her.

She felt ripped wide-open. As if he'd wheeled in a giant spotlight and aimed it directly at her, so bright she could feel the heat of the light itself.

"If you are afraid, there is no shame in admitting it," Thor said in that same surprisingly gentle way she would have said he didn't have, which somehow made her feelings of exposure worse.

"Do I need to be afraid?"

"I would never dream of telling you what you need—lest I be accused of single-handedly imposing the will of the patriarchy upon you."

She glared at him, and at that dry way he talked about the things she'd spent years studying and considering and immersing herself in as if they were so much teenaged caterwauling.

"I would suggest that you view this as a test, nothing more."

Margot didn't tell him that she had always been excellent at tests. "What am I meant to be testing? How much I trust you?"

"I think the fact that you are here, naked and alone in my rooms, speaks to how much you trust me already." And there was nothing threatening in the way he said that. It was a simple statement of fact. And still, Margot felt as if he'd dropped a noose around her neck and pulled it tight. "In any case, this is not about me. It is about you."

"How convenient for you."

"Professor, you don't have to do anything you don't want to do. You never have to do anything you don't want to do. I thought we covered this already when we experimented with consent in the other room. Repeatedly."

"I can assure you that I never, ever do a single thing I don't want to do."

He didn't point out, again, that she was naked and alone with him and had already done things she really ought to be ashamed of. But he didn't need to when Margot was capable of doing it herself, did he?

"What I think is that you do want to do this," he said instead, with all that maddening, seductive patience. "And more, I think the fact you want to put this gag in your own mouth and see what it teaches you, that the very idea makes you wet and greedy, is what scares you most."

Her body was on his side, not hers. Her pussy swelled at his words, and she felt her own wet heat on her thighs.

Damn him.

"It amazes me that you think you can know anything about another person on so short an acquaintance," Margot said loftily, because she didn't know how to do anything but fight. "We are strangers. A state of undress doesn't change the fact that you don't know anything about me."

Thor smiled. "Here is what I know. You cannot bear to let a challenge go unmet, no matter what it costs you. You will force yourself to do things that make you uncomfortable rather than risk losing face. You concentrate on the task set before you, simply because it has been set before you, rather than look inward to see whether or not you want to do it at all."

Margot stiffened. He didn't know her life. He didn't know all the committees she sat on at the university when she wasn't on sabbatical, all because she didn't know how to say no. He didn't know how many papers she'd agreed to coauthor for the same reasons. He couldn't possibly know that when she was so stressed out she thought that ache in her shoulders might never go away, she knew full well she had no one to blame but herself and her own stubbornness.

All he knew about her was how to find her clit. Not a bad skill to have. But not exactly psychic powers, either.

"I complete tasks because that's what adults do, generally speaking," she said. From between her teeth. "It's part of not being a coddled child. The alternative is leaving tasks undone, and *that* leads to chaos, in my experience. Maybe you like having the power turned off because you forgot to take the time to complete the simple task of paying the bill. I don't."

"You didn't have to remove your clothes simply because I asked you to." Thor was studying her again, that fierce blue gaze of his seeing far too much. "I asked you to prove something to me and you did. But why did you do it? Why should you have to prove anything? You could simply have said what you wanted, enthusiastically and repeatedly. But it made you feel safer to have an adversary, did it not?"

She felt dizzy. He might as well have kicked her, hard, in the solar plexus. It took her a long, desperate moment to catch her breath. "I don't think that's true at all."

"But you do think that wanting to experiment with things that have overtones that humorless people take great pleasure in excavating for evidence of wrongdoing makes you weak, somehow. I saw the expression on your face when I suggested that you turn your mouth off for a while. It intrigues you as much as it terrifies you." Thor's smile hurt her. It actually hurt. "You pride yourself on your mind and your mouth, do you not? Who are you if you cannot express yourself exactly as you wish, whenever you wish it? Are you afraid you will cease to exist? I can assure you, my suspicious professor—you will not."

She felt as if she couldn't breathe, but she knew that she could. That she was. She could feel her own chest rise and fall too rapidly. She could hear the ragged sound of her own breath, telling him everything he needed to know without her having to form a single word.

Proving him right.

"I don't think…" she began.

"But that is what we are arguing about. You are not a brain in a jar, Margot. What you think is not independent of your flesh. Your passion. One cannot destroy the other, no matter how hard you try."

"I don't understand what you get out of this. Is it simply that you enjoy the act of humbling—" She almost said *women*, then. But something in the way he watched her kept her from it. "Do you want to humble me? Is that what this is about?"

"I don't want to humble you."

"Then what? Why?"

"I like the things that sex can do above and beyond the act itself. I don't think it's a game. I don't think you can research it the way you might a cell or a virus. Humans are deeply complex and emotional creatures, are we not? Sometimes, if we push our own boundaries, we discover things we never knew were there."

"I have to tell you, Thor. That doesn't sound anything like a handshake."

He smiled anew at that, then took her hand as if he meant to shake it, though he didn't.

"Are you finished talking?" he asked quietly. "Or do you have more nerves to work through?"

Margot knew she had to do it. She had to try, anyway.

She knew other things, too. Such as the fact that somehow, though it shouldn't have been possible, this man really had discovered things about her without benefit of the usual narratives she told about what she liked and didn't like. About who she was or wasn't.

How had he seen all of that? How had sex given him that sort of key to her?

It made her feel restless deep inside.

But when all she wanted to do was open her mouth

and comment on that, extensively and possibly with footnotes, she knew she was stalling.

She made herself reach over and take the napkin from him. And if he saw the way her hand shook, he didn't mention it, proving yet again how unexpectedly kind he was.

It burned through her with its own kind of heat.

It sank down into her bones. It shivered through her, like the blood in her veins. It made her want to cry.

She almost lost her courage, then.

Why are you doing this? that part of her she'd always considered her most rational demanded. *Why are you submitting yourself to something like this?*

But she wanted to see.

She wanted to know.

And Thor stood there before her, that patient intensity illuminating his bright blue gaze and tearing her up inside in too many ways to count.

As if this wasn't about the storm and never had been, but was about Margot herself—and he could wait forever if that was what it took.

It astounded her how much safer she felt when her gaze connected with his and held.

Or better yet, when approval flashed over his lean, fierce face.

Margot rolled the napkin into a long, thin tube, concentrating perhaps a little too hard on making it even. Then she lifted it to her mouth, took a deep breath and fit the napkin between her teeth like some kind of bit for a horse.

She wouldn't call it *surrender*. She wasn't certain she wanted that word in her vocabulary.

But either way, she caught the blue in his eyes. She felt all of that dark intent like his hands around her neck, a perfect storm in the form of a necklace she doubted she'd ever take off, and Margot stopped fighting.

She took a deep breath…and let go.

CHAPTER SEVEN

SHE WAS SO beautiful it hurt.

So brave it didn't merely make his cock hard, it made him worry that he didn't have the control he knew he needed to do this thing.

Because Thor knew that he needed to do it properly if he wanted to do it at all.

He fought to find his center. To calm himself down by focusing on her instead of that greedy fist of need that had him entirely too close to the edge already.

Because she might look at him with those bright gold eyes of hers lit with suspicion, but she trusted him. Although they had never met before tonight, he wasn't the only one who no longer felt as if they were strangers. As if they had never really been strangers.

As if she was more to him in ways he wasn't sure he liked.

It was such an odd sort of intimacy, but Thor didn't fight it. Because she had put that gag in her mouth for no other reason than that he'd suggested it.

She trusted him.

Not because she knew him or really anything about him. Not because she'd heard enough rumors about him from random people in Reykjavík to form a sketchy opinion that might allow her to engage in a quick, meaningless fuck. Not because he was Daniel St. George's eldest illegitimate son and somehow the most accessible of the lot—or so it seemed to Thor when the three of them had their stilted, careful conversations, as ordered by the father none of them had known or liked all that much.

Margot might have known a few broad details about Thor, the way everyone did since the will had come out and made him an international person of interest instead of merely one of Iceland's relatively few celebrities. But none of that was why she was willing to trust him tonight.

None of that was why she was standing before him, her eyes wide and that napkin distorting the shape of her lovely mouth.

She trusted him because of what had happened here, over the course of this deliciously endless night. She trusted him because he hadn't told her who he was, he'd shown her.

And now he had the opportunity to show her who *she* was, too.

It was a privilege.

Margot was breathing hard and a little too fast through her nose, and he could see the sheen of glassiness that made her eyes gleam ever more gold. Her hands kept forming into fists at her sides, then releasing. Over and over, as if she was *this close* to bolting.

But she didn't balk. She didn't break.

And when he reached over to liberate that wrap from around her shoulders, the only reaction he got was the faintest, finest little tremor snaking down her torso before she squared her shoulders and repressed it.

Out in the main, rambling room of his penthouse that he liked because it told visitors nothing about him, she looked like the finest of the art he collected and hung in the house he kept in the city. Except better. More precious.

Thor stood back from her and took a moment to admire her. All that fine, flushed skin. The upturned pink of her nipples, the strawberry blond curls between her legs. And the lavender hair that fell all around her, cascading over her shoulders in a kind of artless invitation.

And she trusted him.

It was enough to make him lose it right there, but he didn't.

Somehow, he didn't.

He took her hand and led her out from the seating area where they'd eaten, closer to the enormous fireplace that was built into one sleek wall and looked as if the fire rose directly from the decorative volcanic rock. But he didn't stop there. He kept moving until they stood before the giant window that in good weather looked out over the brooding sea. Tonight it would be much too dark and stormy to see anything even if he'd had all the lights on.

Which he didn't. So what he saw when he looked at his window was Margot's reflection in the glass and, here and there, hints of the driving snow outside.

He stood behind her for a moment, soaking in the view.

He could also see that Margot didn't like it. He saw the way her brows drew together, and that snap in her gaze when it met his in the glass.

"See?" he murmured, snaking an arm around her middle to haul her closer to him and enjoying the feel of her, silky and warm. He held her with her back flush against his front so she could feel his heat. His strength. His greedy cock in the small of her back. "Your nonverbal communication comes across loud and clear. You do not want to look at yourself like this. You do not want to be on display. No doubt you have some concerns about objectification."

Her nostrils flared slightly. Then, slowly, she nodded.

Thor brushed her hair away from her neck on one side and bent to taste her there, sweet and hot.

"Perhaps it is time we talk about the differences between objectification and admiration," he said, right there against her skin where he could taste the way she trembled. "You assume that being on display makes you less, somehow, when we raise our gods and our icons high, the better to adore them. We elevate the things we cherish. We create pedestals, cathedrals, museums. Why should it be any different between lovers?"

He put his hands on her skin, running one palm over that tattoo on her side that declared her persistence. And he moved the other higher on her rib cage until it rested just below her breast, and tried not to let the sight right there in the window before them roar through him unchecked, because he wasn't sure he'd be able to keep himself under control if it did.

"You were so concerned about power dynamics earlier," he continued. "But ask yourself this. Did I give you orders or make suggestions? And if I did issue an order, why are you focusing on the order rather than your need to follow it? Is it problematic if you want to do it or only if you think I want you to do it?"

He studied her face and that frown she still wore, though her teeth were clenched down hard on the napkin. He wasn't sure he'd ever seen anything prettier or more compelling than Margot fighting her need to tear that napkin from her mouth and light into him with all those mighty words she knew.

But it was his turn to do the talking.

"If we are two consenting adults and we both get something out of a power dynamic, why must it be considered problematic at all?" he asked. "Why do you imagine you get to decide how it is that other people get off in the first place?"

She made a little noise of protest and he smiled. "It seems to me that if a woman tells you that she enjoys submission, as you claim you do not, you are the one who is infantilizing her if you decide that the only way she can enjoy such things is if she has somehow betrayed herself. Or does not know her own mind sufficiently to make that determination. If a woman tells you that she is no victim but you decide that you know better, who is truly victimizing her?"

Thor didn't glance toward her face to see if he could divine her answer from her expression. He didn't need to. He could feel the way she trembled in his hands. He indulged himself instead, shifting his palm so he could cover one of those velvety nipples that stood there, pink and proud.

He moved his palm in slow, lazy circles and kept his mouth at her neck.

"I think that no matter how you try to politicize sex or what good intentions you might have for doing it, all you truly end up doing is judging personal preference. And my suggestion to you, Professor, is that personal preference is none of your business."

And he punctuated that thought by finding her hot, wet pussy with his free hand.

He could hear the moans she made in her throat,

sweet and needy. He could feel that same neediness in a rush of damp heat against his fingers.

Thor stroked her folds, gently playing with her clit. Almost as if it was an afterthought, and her hips moved as if of their own accord in time to his every light, teasing stroke. Her hands fisted and released at her sides.

Again and again.

"All this research you do. All these papers you write. All the many ways you try to convince yourself that this isn't real." He put his mouth to her ear and it was as if he could taste her arousal, all that delirious heat. He made his strokes longer, lazier, and felt the way her hips hitched. "Does it feel real now?"

She made another noise. Frustration. Helpless need. Thor reached over to take one of those convulsive little hands in his, then drew it between her legs.

And had the particular delight of feeling her freeze. Then bloom with heat.

Everywhere.

"Feel yourself. Your pussy doesn't lie, Margot." He was teaching her a lesson, and yet it was the first time he hadn't called her *Professor*. And that seemed to strike an odd little note in him, a ringing like a bell that seemed to move in all his limbs at once, but he shoved it aside. "You're either wet or you are not. Your pussy knows exactly what it wants. And it has no compunction about telling you. Feel your wetness.

Feel how you quiver. Your body knows what it needs, what it desires. It is only you who are confused."

She made another one of those angry, frustrated sounds and he smiled, there in the crook of her shoulder where she could feel it.

"If you could talk, would you tell me that you are not confused at all? I think you would. But that's the trouble with words. They are indirect. They stretch across feelings and analyze them, contain them, change them in the telling. Your body is more direct. Uncompromising, you might say. There's a certain purity in a hard cock and a wet pussy. Everything else is a complication. Everything else is what we put on it, not what it is."

He slid his fingers over hers, there in all her slickness, and showed her exactly what he wanted her to do.

"Make yourself come," he ordered her, his voice like a growl. "And the beauty of the gag in your mouth is that you cannot tell me if that's possible or impossible. You can only do it."

She made another noise, but it wasn't a word. He wasn't sure it was even an attempt at words. He lifted his head so he could see the look of flushed frustration on her face in the window, and that ever-present frown of hers that he found he'd begun to crave. She looked as if she wanted to object. To argue.

But the truth was in that hand beneath his, buried between her thighs. She rocked her palm against her clit and she didn't stop. She didn't even pause, no matter how she scowled at him.

"The more you think, the less you feel," Thor told her, his gaze fused to hers in the reflection before them. "And if you are talking, you cannot be listening. So this is my challenge to you, Professor. Stop thinking. Stop talking—especially to yourself. Lose yourself in this."

And for a while there was nothing but the sound of her breath and the soft sound of her hand working between her legs.

Thor played with her nipple. He watched her face. "It either feels good or doesn't. You will either come or you won't. Does your body know what it wants? And if it does, do you give it what it wants or do you deny it out of some misplaced notion of what you *ought* to like?"

Her breathing was heavy. He couldn't tell if it was frustration or something else now, but either way, she didn't stop. He stood there behind her, the scent of her heavy in the air between them. It was a musky female arousal and a sharp, full vanilla that was all Margot. He wanted to taste her. He wanted to lift her up, tip her forward and settle her on his own aching cock at last.

But he waited, though he thought the waiting might kill him. He shifted to move his hands over her curves instead. As if he was settling and soothing her as much as he was attempting to excite her. He traced the span of her hips. He smoothed his palms up her sides, then along her arms.

He explored her as if he was committing her to memory, stroke by stroke.

And all the while she fucked herself with her hand, rolling her hips to meet her own palm.

Thor got to watch that delicious flush spread out over her skin, from the sweet triangle of her coppery curls to her lavender hair that fell down all around her, teasing the tips of her breasts. Her eyes drifted closed. Her head lolled back against his shoulder.

"Come," he ordered her, low and gritty. "Come, Professor. Now."

And when she obeyed him, it was like a tempest shook through her. He found himself gripping her hips to hold her steady. To keep her on her feet. Or better yet, to keep her from toppling over where she stood.

She shook and she shook. And when the shaking subsided, her hand dropped from between her thighs and she slid, boneless and still breathing hard, against him.

Thor turned her around in his arms, then picked her up and carried her over to the thick rug before the fire. He dropped to his knees and set her on hers.

And then he took his time and a good deal of care pushing her hair back from her face. He tucked the damp lavender strands behind her ears. And he didn't know what to call that weighty, complicated, knot-

ted thing that squatted there in his chest and refused
to be dislodged.

He didn't know what to call the urges that rolled
through him then, none of them about the heavy
need in his cock. None of them about pounding his
way to oblivion.

The trouble with teaching lessons was that he
couldn't avoid learning a few of his own while he
did it.

And one of them was the simple fact that this
woman was nothing like the many other women Thor
had enjoyed in his past. He was too…involved. He
was obsessed with that mouth he wasn't allowed to
kiss. He was entirely too invested in the things he
wanted to show her. About herself. About the pair
of them. About sex itself. But he wasn't as removed
as he usually was. He couldn't seem to find his footing or his usual distance.

Something about Margot was lodging its way
deep inside him whether he liked it or not. As if
she was leaving scars he wasn't entirely sure would
ever heal.

Worse, he must have liked it. Because he wasn't
doing a thing to stop it.

Especially when Margot pulled the napkin from
her mouth. She made a face as she ran her tongue
around inside her own mouth, tossing the bit of cloth
to the side.

"Dry?" he asked, feeling as close to desperate as he'd ever been.

Because he wasn't used to this...*wanting*. He hadn't lied to her. Icelanders fucked. He certainly did and it had always been fun. Sometimes an intense kind of fun.

But it had never been like this, as if she was stripping away layers of his skin every time she met his gaze. Every time she frowned at him. Every time she came in that pink rush.

Even though she'd removed her gag, Margot didn't speak. She blinked once, then again, as if she was getting her bearings. And when she lifted her gaze to meet his, the gold in them was so brilliant he nearly looked away.

She was flushed and she was fierce and he wanted her in ways he didn't understand. He wanted to fuck her. He wanted to lose himself in her. He wanted *her*, all of her. Not just her nakedness, but every complicated thought in that fascinating head of hers.

She was breaking all his rules.

Margot reached over, put her hands on his chest and didn't say a word as she pushed him backward.

Thor could have fought her, of course, but he saw no reason to do such a thing. Not when he could fall back against the rug and let her climb over him and surrender himself to part of what he wanted.

He kept expecting her to say something. To challenge him in that way of hers. To analyze what had already happened and throw her buzzwords at him in that way she did.

Because he craved that, too.

But it seemed that she had taken his advice to heart, because she didn't say a word.

She simply…helped herself to his body as if he was the object.

Or, if he corrected himself, as if he was what she admired.

And she took her sweet time admiring him.

She used her mouth all over his chest. Her mouth and her hands and the seductive sweep of that lavender hair. She tasted him and she teased him, licking her way over his nipples and then tracing the outline of his pectoral muscles. She knelt beside him and explored each arm, and each leg, the way he'd done. She tugged off his loose trousers and threw them aside, and then she started all over again.

She kissed him everywhere except his cock and his mouth, and by the time she crawled back up the length of him and threw herself down beside him, Thor thought he might go out of his mind. He worried he already had. He thought his skin might crack wide-open with the force of his need—

And the only way he knew how to handle it was to get inside her.

Even though he already understood it wouldn't be enough.

She still hadn't said a word.

"Have you gone mute?" he gritted out, his control a pale shadow of what it ought to have been. He knew that, and even if he hadn't, he could hear it. He couldn't tell if it was anger or anguish or some passionate form of torment in between the two, but he couldn't keep it in. It spilled out of him as if of its own accord.

And the crazy part was, he couldn't seem to bring himself to care about that the way he should have. The way he knew he would, if he survived.

"Tell me what you want," she demanded, her voice husky from disuse.

And more, with something else that it took him long moments to realize was a kind of sheer, humming power that resonated inside him like the towering wall of the ferocious North Atlantic over a black sand beach.

Like home.

"You," he growled. "Now."

"You have to be more specific," she told him, and even though her lips curved, there was still that fierceness, a kind of wickedness that made every part of his body pull tight and hard.

She was a goddess. Gold and purple, flushed sweet cream.

Thor was lost.

"I need you beneath me, Margot," he managed to grit out.

He didn't know which one of them moved then,

only that they were flipping around until he was on top of her at last, pressing himself into that sweet cradle between her legs.

They were both blessedly naked. And for a moment Thor held himself there, enjoying the simple perfection of her bare skin against his. The way his cock notched into her soft heat.

The anticipation.

"I'm beneath you," Margot said in that same demanding, daring way that lit him up everywhere they touched. And everywhere they didn't. "Now what?"

"I am not the one who hides behind words," he said, though everything in him shouted for him to simply tilt his hips, find her slick entrance and bury himself in her pussy at last. "Do you think I need to learn the same lessons?"

"I think that you're so certain you don't need to learn a thing that it probably means you do," Margot replied simply, that powerful current running through her and into him.

And the fact she was saying something he didn't want to hear didn't change that electricity.

If anything, it turned a simple charge into a lightning strike.

"I already told you. I'm fluent in all kinds of languages. My body isn't a mystery to me, Margot."

And as if he had to prove it, right there and then, he thrust himself deep inside her.

She groaned. He did, too. And for a moment the

pleasure was so intense, almost excruciating, it was as if they had to freeze to survive the impact of it.

Thor held himself above her, his palms braced against the ground on either side of her head. And Margot was a flushed tangle of purple hair and bright eyes beneath him.

"But you have no issues, of course," Margot murmured, her voice soft but still infused with that note of power that made him think of the sea. "You have no needs. You're near perfect, just as you are."

There were a thousand things Thor could have said then, but he didn't. He pulled out, taking his time in making certain he dragged the head of his cock over all the parts of her he could, there in that tight channel where he'd already found each and every place that made her shiver. He found them all again. He reminded them both how well he fit. Then he thrust himself back in.

But Margot was still talking. "It's perfectly normal to run a hotel like this. To live in an antiseptic penthouse that echoes when you walk. You have no daddy issues at all. If we opened up a dictionary right this minute, we would find your picture next to the word *well-adjusted*. I'm certain of it."

He knew she was taunting him. And he thought he should stop it. Or counter it, anyway. He certainly couldn't allow it to go unchallenged—

But he didn't use words. He thought words were beside the point.

He used the deep thrust, then the slow drag out. He used the angle of his hips and the way he moved them. He used the intensity of his pace and the way he could alter it at will to throw her toward the edge and then keep her there.

And keep her there.

She laughed, breathless and more than a little bit wild. And then she braced her hands on his chest as if that could stop this. As if anything could stop this.

"Here's what I know about you, Thor," Margot said, and her voice was thicker now. He could hear the little breaths that caught in her throat every time he surged deep within her, but she didn't stop. "You like to talk. You claim to be about the body, but the truth is that it's all mind games, isn't it? The only question I have is—who are you playing those games for, me or you?"

He shifted, going down on his elbows so he could press the wall of his chest against the glory of her breasts and make it all ache that much more.

"You're so cool. So aloof. You claim you listen to your body, but even while you fuck you're analyzing. Cataloging." Her gaze was a blaze of gold. "No wonder sex is your favorite form of recreation. You don't have to worry about true intimacy when everything is so clinical."

Thor didn't tell her what he thought about her sudden abiding interest in intimacy. He showed her. He picked up his pace, moving just fast enough so that she hitched up her knees on either side of him, putting her feet flat on the rug to give herself a little purchase to lift up and meet each thrust.

"You live in a sex hotel. You have this stark and empty penthouse all to yourself. You're so busy building walls around yourself that you don't even know you're doing it. Nothing can touch you. No one can know you. The more available you make yourself, the less you can be seen. But I see you."

Her voice broke then. And Thor wasn't thinking. He wasn't sure he was listening so much as he was withstanding the way each word she said burned into him, and scorched him deep inside.

And all the while he was lost in that sweet, delirious slide. He couldn't tell anymore if he was keeping to a pace or if he was simply losing himself inside her.

He couldn't tell if he was lost.

And he didn't care.

"I see you, Thor," she whispered again, and then everything was fire. There was a blistering light that ate them both alive, an electric madness that he didn't know whether to crave or fear.

He did neither. Both. He pounded into her and she met him, and he couldn't tell who was fucking who.

It was as if they were moving parts of the same whole, making a blistering storm all their own.

He felt her shake again, and he knew her now. He knew the way she came apart. He knew that tight, hot clench of her pussy around his cock. The way her thighs clamped down on the outside of his. The way she lifted herself to take more of him, all of him, arching her back to press herself even more firmly against him.

And Thor kept going. He fucked her through one orgasm, then straight on into another.

It was too hot. It was too *right*. He believed that she could see him and more, worse, he could see himself at last.

And when he released himself inside her, he knew beyond a shadow of a doubt that he was lost.

The trouble was, he understood as he heard himself shout out her name and tumble off into the madness of that storm they'd built, he didn't think he wanted to be found.

CHAPTER EIGHT

MARGOT WOKE SLOWLY, a delicious sort of warmth all over her.

It took her a long moment, then another, to understand where she was.

Iceland. Thor Ragnarsson's famous sex hotel. Trapped at the notorious Hotel Viking by a blizzard, no less.

Which meant she'd actually survived the most intense night of her life.

She opened her eyes and found herself out on one of the low, wide couches in the main room in Thor's stark penthouse. She could hear his voice, though she couldn't see him from where she lay, sprawled out on the sofa that could have fit them both—and had, if she wasn't mistaken. She shifted, realizing as she did that he had tucked her under a thick duvet and that was what was keeping her toasty warm despite the fact she was still naked.

Margot sat up slowly, blinking as she looked around. There was still snow on the other side of the large windows, but the difference was that she could see light out there as well. Far more light, anyway, than she had seen since yesterday morning in Reykjavík.

It took her a moment to find Thor. He was far away, down at the other end of the great space in what she quickly realized must have been his office. He was speaking on the phone in rapid Icelandic, standing with his back to her and his gaze out at the storm.

He had dressed. More than simply dressed. He was wearing the kind of suit that made it perfectly clear that he was a man of international clout. It was dark and cut to flatter, making him look taller, somehow. More beautiful, if such a thing was possible. He held one hand on the top of his head, as if he'd started to rake it through his blond hair but had forgotten to complete the action.

And Margot was fiercely, fervently glad that he couldn't see her. That she had a moment without that piercing blue stare of his boring into her. That she could take a breath or two to compose herself. Hell, to *remember* herself. To try to put the jumble of thoughts and sensation into some kind of order without knowing he was watching her do it.

She had only the vaguest memories of what had happened there before the fire after that last, intense round of this game that didn't feel anything like a game at all. She had no idea how long they'd lain there together. She'd been slightly aware when he'd moved them to the couch, and she knew that he had slept there with her for some time. She had no memory of him leaving her, and even less of him covering her up.

She was almost certain it was morning, though she supposed it could be later on into the day, with all that snow.

Margot felt like a different person.

She found her fingers on her mouth, as if she expected to feel bruised there. But she thought that really, if there were any marks, they would be inside her. She felt torn apart. Rearranged.

Changed beyond recognition.

She pulled the duvet more tightly around her and took stock of her body, realizing with an uneasy sort of sensation that even her own limbs didn't feel like hers any longer.

Margot had dedicated her life to the pursuit of knowledge, but Thor had taught her—over and over and over again—how very little she knew about something as basic and fundamental as sex.

She'd spent her adult life studying something she had never experienced—not really, not like this or anything near *this*—and she suspected that, given time, she would find that horrifying. And maybe also sad.

She felt too many things, all at once, and her experience with that damned napkin had already taught her too well.

She didn't try to interpret them. She didn't try to analyze them.

It was as if they rolled through her, one wave and then the next. A deep kind of regret that she had never known what she was missing. That she had been so certain she was in the position to lecture on the topic of sex in the first place when all the sex she had ever had before had been so…deficient. There was an exultant kind of exhilaration that her body could do those things. That she could feel those things. That she was capable of so much she hadn't even known was possible.

Looking at Thor made her sad. Furious. Giddy. And so silly that she could feel a smile on her mouth for absolutely no reason at all.

One wave and then the next.

She felt ashamed that it had taken a gag in her mouth to teach her how to find her voice. She had a picture of herself in her head, that napkin in her mouth and her hand between her legs, and she felt it, too. The memory turned her on even as it made something in her stomach turn over, as if she thought she ought to find it sickening. But mostly it just made her hot all over again.

She *felt*.

And Margot had no earthly idea how she was ever going to manage to put these things she felt into any kind of order. How she was ever to make sense of them.

Thor finished his conversation and tossed his phone on the desk that spread there across the whole of one wall in a kind of nook that prevented her from seeing his numerous screens straight on. He didn't turn around. He stayed where he was, staring out the window, and Margot thought she would give anything at all to see the expression on his face.

But when he turned, she had the sense that he'd known that she was awake and watching him all along, because his expression was wiped clean.

For a moment they only stared at each other, all the rambling, empty space of the penthouse between them.

Margot thought there was a whole lot more distance than that. And more, she could feel it gape wider and more impassable inside her the longer they did nothing but…look at each other.

When his phone rang again, it was a relief.

Thor held her gaze for a long moment. The ringing continued, but he didn't move to answer anything and she wasn't sure what she saw in his face. It wasn't as simple as resignation. His eyes were too blue for that. And she was sure that all that aloofness she'd noticed before was different now.

Everything is different now, something intoned, deep inside her.

His phone kept ringing.

"I have to take this," he told her, almost stiffly, in a voice that didn't sound loud at all and yet managed to echo down the length of the great room.

Margot inclined her head as if she was giving him her permission. And she could see Thor didn't like it. If she were a better person, she would have offered to remove herself to the next room while he handled his business.

But this was the man who'd encouraged her to put a fucking napkin in her mouth.

"Intimacy takes many forms, doesn't it?" she replied, also pitching her voice to carry. "It's really the gift that keeps on giving."

She saw temper flash across Thor's face, but he didn't argue with her any further. He turned back to his office and rummaged for something on his desktop. Not that anyone would have known it was the desktop. Margot hadn't seen the desk before, and it took her perhaps too long to realize that was because it was the sort of desk that could be hidden away in a cabinet. Imagine that. A whole life that could be easily tucked away from prying eyes whenever the mood took him.

It seemed she knew more about Thor than she'd realized. That she had been right on target, in fact.

Margot waited to feel a surge of triumph, but it was something else that moved in her, making her feel a little too close to a man who was standing as far away as it was possible to get from her while still being in the same sprawling penthouse.

"It's angled," Thor said, which made no sense. "You're not in the frame."

She didn't understand that, or why he hadn't answered that ringing, but then the huge, flat screen on the wall behind his desk area bloomed into life and color.

"Why do you always look like you're standing in a fucking morgue?" came a low, raspy voice with an American accent. Not just a random, unplaceable American accent that could have been from anywhere, but one laced with hints of the South and a faint, dirty drawl.

Margot sank down on the couch, suddenly entirely too aware that Thor was *on a video call* and she was naked. Covered up in a comforter, sure. Out of frame, he'd said. But she was naked all the same, and that felt…wrong when there was another voice. And when it sounded like *that*.

"I assume you mean that my Nordic sensibilities offend you," Thor was saying in reply.

And he sounded…not quite like the man she thought she'd come to know over the course of a night that Margot felt had lasted several lifetimes already. Something scraped at her, thick and insistent, and she realized that he sounded like the Thor she had met downstairs last night. There in the bar, when he'd come up behind her and she'd thought he was nothing but another hotel guest. Who'd been attempting to hit on her.

It made her feel a little dizzy to think about how different things were now. How much a single night had changed them both.

"Sensibilities don't offend me, brother," the same voice replied.

"Aloha, motherfuckers," a third voice chimed in then. Richer, darker. And with a lilting sort of hint of an accent that Margot found unfamiliar but assumed went along with the Hawaiian greeting.

She peeked her head up over the back of the couch to sneak a look at the screen, hoping she really was out of frame. She assumed she must have been when no one said anything, and that allowed her to study the screen. It was split in two. On one side sat a very large, gorgeously muscled man bathed in sunlight with palm trees and blue water behind him. His eyebrows were arched and jet black, a fascinating contrast to his brown skin and the smirk on his surprisingly lush mouth. His black hair fell around his face, a little too long to Margot's way of thinking. A little too messy.

He wasn't beautiful, but he was purely carnal. Margot was surprised he didn't sizzle.

She was surprised she didn't, simply from looking at him.

The man on the other side of the screen was blond, though a darker, dirtier blond than Thor. He was

also built out of lean, hard muscles and razor-sharp
lines, like those fascinating cheekbones of his. And
maybe it was his similarities to Thor that clued her
in: his blue eyes, though a darker, moodier blue than
Thor's; a tilt to his head that suggested he was up to
no particular good; the kind of mouth that made Margot's mind seem to go blank for a whole beat or two.

She understood that these must be Thor's half
brothers. Thor's famous half brothers, made objects
of international interest the moment their existence
had been confirmed at the reading of Daniel St.
George's will six months ago.

Her heart thudded a little too hard for her peace of
mind, but it wasn't because Thor's half brothers were
so ridiculously attractive. It was because Thor himself looked so...stern and disapproving as he glared
at his screen.

"I thought *aloha* was a Hawaiian thing," the blond
with the drawl said.

He was Charlie Teller, if Margot remembered her
research into Thor correctly. The article she'd read
about Daniel St. George's long-lost sons had made
vague references to Charlie's brushes with the law
and potentially dangerous associates. He didn't look
dangerous on screen—or he didn't *only* look dangerous. He was grinning broadly, tipped back in a chair
in a room somewhere. With terra-cotta walls that
struck Margot as...insistent, somehow.

"It is a Hawaiian thing. *I'm* a Hawaiian thing."

That third voice was Jason Kaoki. She'd read
about him, too. A local Pacific Island boy turned
good, the fawning article had called him. He had
gone off to college on the mainland on a full foot-
ball scholarship and had even played a few years pro
before sustaining the kind of injuries that had forced
him into early retirement. He was rumored to be a
major, if anonymous, philanthropist in Hawaii and
other Pacific Islands. And then had come the will.

"You're not actually in Hawaii, though, are you?"
Charlie asked. "I thought you were on some random
ass island out there in the middle somewhere."

"Are you trying to throw down with me about
some Pacific Island shit, you haole fuck?" Jason
demanded, then belted out a big, broad laugh that
seemed to warm up even this cavernous room where
Margot lay, far across the planet from his light and
sea and palm trees, surrounded by snow and ice.

And a chilly Thor besides.

"As delightful as this questionable camaraderie
is," Thor interjected coolly then, as if he could hear
Margot's thoughts, "I believe this is meant to be a
business call, is it not?"

"I'd tell you to chill out, brother," Charlie said,
and Margot wondered if she was the only one who
heard the sardonic kick in the way he used that word.
Brother. "But I'm not sure that Viking ass could get
any colder."

Jason laughed again and it had the same effect as

before. Bright and loud, as if he didn't have a care in the world and didn't care what the idiots on his screen were talking about.

Though Margot imagined it would be a very foolish person indeed who failed to note the clever gleam in his dark gaze.

"I find Viking commentary entertaining," Thor said. "I do. But these conversations are supposed to be about money."

"I like money," Jason said, and he still sounded as merry. As lazy. "But how much can any one man have?"

"Meaning you're still holding out," Charlie replied, as if that was a code. "You might as well surrender, brother. The long arm of Daniel St. George reaches from beyond the grave whether you want it to or not. You can tell yourself whatever lies you want, but believe me, you're going to end up building that hotel."

Jason smiled, big and broad, but Margot was caught on the shrewd look in his gaze.

"You had a lot of good reasons to leave the mainland. I'm assuming Italy was one of those reasons. Maybe your life choices on the mainland were another reason." Jason shrugged as if it was no matter to him. As if he couldn't see the way Charlie's smile became indefinably more dangerous. "But I like my island the way it is."

"Jason is still holding off on development plans.

How is the Amalfi Coast treating you?" Thor asked Charlie with no particular inflection in his cool voice.

"Italian, Thor. It seems really fucking Italian."

There was more laughter, though somehow, it didn't surprise Margot that Thor didn't join in.

"Everything continues apace here in Iceland," Thor told them. "Business is booming."

"Sex always sells," Charlie said with a shrug. "And water is wet, the sun comes up in the east and a douchebag is what a douchebag does."

"Is that life advice?" Jason asked.

"I'm a life coach in my spare time," Charlie drawled.

"We could all say a great many things about the man, certainly," Thor said, an edge in his voice that made goose bumps prickle along Margot's arms— and also cut through his half brothers' laughter. "But our father always had excellent taste in hotels."

"Don't call that asshole our father," Charlie muttered. "Jesus."

"He's nothing to me but one more haole," Jason said, which Margot interpreted as his agreement.

"I'm thrilled we agree on something," Thor said. "I'll send the usual email outlining our continued progress in our respective areas. Duty calls, gentlemen. Next week?"

"Next week," Charlie said with that same smile

that the longer Margot looked at it, the less she thought was all that nice. "Every fucking week."

"Aloha, bitches," Jason said merrily.

And then there was silence when the screen went dark.

Margot stayed where she was. She was frowning toward the windows closest to her, shifting pieces around in her head, and it took her a moment to notice when Thor came to stand behind the couch. Next to her, but separated by the back of the couch.

And yet even though he had moved closer, it was as if he was on the other end of one of those video cameras. He looked as remote as if he'd carved himself from ice.

He made her feel shivery inside in a way that had nothing to do with sex, but felt a lot more as if she might tip over into tears at any moment. That closed-down look on his face made her hurt.

"Are you okay?" she asked quietly.

He looked startled, but only for a moment. Then it was straight back to ice and stone, shuttered and forbidding.

"It is a stipulation of the contracts we signed to take over the hotels our father left us that we hold these pointless conversations." He didn't sound like the man who had spent a long night weaving spells around Margot with his words alone. He sounded almost stilted. The way he had while he'd talked on his call. "Weekly."

"Does it stipulate that you have to be best friends on all those calls?" Margot pushed herself up, until she could cross her legs beneath her and sit up straight. "Either way, they didn't sound particularly awful."

"They are not awful. They are perfectly fine, I suppose, for full-grown men I am apparently related to and must now interact with as if we have some kind of history." Thor shook his head, but it was more as if he was shaking something off. "I do not understand brothers."

Margot thought that what he couldn't understand was connection, however new and strange, but she didn't say that. She didn't think it was the sort of thing he could hear at the moment. And probably not from her as she sat there, still sure she could taste that napkin in her mouth. "Have you met them in person?"

"The will was read in Germany." And once Thor said it, Margot remembered that she'd read that, too. The article had shown pictures of a law firm in Hamburg and paparazzi shots of men in dark coats and sunglasses. It was odd to think that she now knew what one of those dark-coated men tasted like. "The only thing more awkward than finding out that your father, who you never met and never wanted to meet, left you property you didn't want after his death is discovering that he did the same to others."

Margot wanted to touch him. She settled for her

hands in fists in the duvet and a smile. "Do you think maybe he wanted all of you to band together and become some kind of family after he was gone?"

Thor laughed, though it was a far hollower sound than the laughter they'd heard from his half brothers. And it seemed to lodge between Margot's ribs. "He would have to have been delusional to imagine such a thing. But then, I think it is fairly clear that he was exactly that or he wouldn't have used his will to perform paternal acts in absentia. So who knows? Maybe this is what he thinks a family is."

"Thor…"

He was still dressed in that glorious dark suit of his and she considered it for a moment. He hadn't been wearing a suit yesterday. In her time in Iceland, come to that, she hadn't seen very many suits at all. They didn't go very well with the weather, for one thing. Which made her wonder why, exactly, Thor had chosen to throw one on this morning when he'd known he had to have this phone call with the half brothers he hardly knew.

She thought she could guess.

The idea that Thor, the strongest and most fascinating man she'd ever met, should feel the need to put on his armor before dealing with his family made a hot, prickling sensation threaten the backs of her eyes. Margot didn't dare let a single drop of moisture fall, but she had to blink a little too quickly to make sure.

And she gripped her duvet tighter.

"They say that a man is not truly a man until he teaches his son the sagas," Thor told her, after a long, taut silence. "I suppose it is another way of talking about fatherhood. But the man who taught me the sagas was my stepfather. Ragnar raised me. He taught me to read. He took care of my mother and me. He was a good man, always. In all my memories of childhood, I cannot recall a single time he drank too much or raised his voice. He was a big, kind, gentle man."

Margot was afraid to ask the next question. She had to force it out. "Is he…?"

"He died years ago, when I was twenty-five. He got a cough that wouldn't go away, and within three months, he was dead."

Margot searched his face and saw nothing. Only stone and ice and something harder still in the blue depths of his gaze.

"I'm so sorry," she said anyway.

"I am not telling you this story for your sympathy," Thor said with a kind of quiet menace that felt a lot like a kick to the gut, but Margot refused to show him that he'd landed a hit. "I always knew who my father was and it was not Daniel St. George. It was never Daniel St. George. I knew that name. I would have given anything not to know that name, but it was unavoidable. I hated him. But I never, not once, considered him my father."

Margot couldn't read him. There was a voice inside her that tasted a lot like panic, and it kept urging her to stop this. To go. To retreat from the tension, take a shower, pretend she couldn't tell that Thor was going through something.

But she couldn't bring herself to do it. "It makes sense to hate the man for leaving you."

Thor's mouth curved, cold and harsh. "You have to acknowledge a child in order to leave it, I think. Daniel St. George never condescended to do any such thing. I think I told you that my mother married Ragnar before I was born. But she never got over Daniel St. George. Never."

He shoved his hands into the pockets of his suit trousers, as if he didn't know what he meant to do with them. A kind of bitterness hung over him, like a cloud. She could see it in his eyes and in the twist of his lips. Worse, she could *feel* it, chilling her skin even though she still sat with the duvet wrapped around her.

"My mother is the one who drinks too much, Professor. And when she does, she cries. She becomes maudlin and bemoans all she has lost. Some might suggest that she lost nothing, but she never got over the man who left her without a second thought all those years ago. She spent the whole of her marriage to my stepfather nursing her broken heart. It was not something she bothered to hide. Her epic, eternal sadness, her inability to love Ragnar back, her grief—this was the third presence in our house. There was no point in making a child of their own because they not only had me, they had their very own ghost."

Margot thought of her own chilly upbringing. The pressure of her father's expectations. The way her mother had bent and contorted and still always proved that she was no match for the man she'd married. Margot's father had long since given up pretending he had anything but contempt for his spouse. And Margot understood now, in a different way than she had when she was younger, that she should be deeply ashamed that she, too, often had followed his lead because she and her mother had been engaged in a sick little competition to win the man's affection and regard.

It wasn't as if she wanted to hold her own family up as any kind of ideal. But there had never been any third parties in her parents' marriage or in the house where Margot had grown up. There had been no ghosts, only regrets.

"Did she ever see Daniel St. George again?" Margot asked gently, carefully. Because she didn't dare call the man Thor's father. She suspected that was a weapon he tolerated only when he wielded it himself.

Thor's gaze was so cold it made Margot's bones ache. "He had no desire to see her again, something that only became clear to her when he died. In many ways, he left her twice. He left her pregnant and alone, and then, all these years later, he left that will so he could slap her down once again by virtue of ignoring her once more. And between you and me, I am not certain she will ever fully recover."

"What do you mean?"

"It seems it took the callousness of the man's will to finally make it clear to my mother what kind of man he was," Thor said, all that bitterness and icy chill making his voice sound different. Almost scratchy. "The newspapers would have you believe that it was an act of kindness. An old man reaching out to the sons he'd abandoned and offering a kind of olive branch from the grave. Perhaps my half brothers think so, I do not know."

"But you don't."

"I think it was one more demonstration of his cruelty." Thor swallowed hard, and Margot had the sense he could hear that scratchiness in his voice. And hated it. "Because his will made it clear he knew exactly who we were and where we had been, all this time. He knew who had raised us and how. He knew the details of our lives, which means he'd been paying attention, all these years. He could have made contact at any point, but didn't. Daniel St. George was interested in one thing only, and that was the perpetuation of his name. Through his sons. He didn't care who he'd made those sons with."

"Thor…"

"And do not deceive yourself. He has no interest

in the daughter he made, either. The only difference between my overlooked half sister and the women my father impregnated and abandoned is that my sister was summoned to the will reading and left an insult. Neither my mother nor anyone else was even mentioned. As far as Daniel St. George was concerned, they never existed."

"He sounds like a very sad, pathetic old man with dynastic pretensions."

Thor raked a hand through his hair, and it seemed he'd lost the battle with the emotion in his voice. It cracked. And it bled through into his blue gaze, too. "Now when my mother drinks, she does not regret the love she lost before I was born. She regrets the love she had all those years afterward that she could never quite accept. She regrets all those maudlin nights she cried for a man who cared nothing for her, while hurting one who did."

Margot hardly knew she meant to move, but then there she was, kneeling up on the couch so she could move herself closer to him. So she could reach out before she thought better of it and put her hands on his body.

She told herself not to pay any attention to that strange disconnection she felt because of it. Because he'd gone so cold overnight when she'd woken up warm all over.

Because she felt as if she knew him so well, and yet didn't know him at all, and she didn't have to have a hundred morning afters like this under her belt to understand that he likely didn't want to hear that.

"Thor," she said softly, amazed to find she could feel his heat through his clothes when she'd expected nothing but cold. "I'm sorry."

"You have nothing to apologize for. You weren't one of the players in this game." He looked down at her hands as if he couldn't make sense of them, there pressed into his sides. "I didn't build this antiseptic penthouse, you call it. I don't live here. This is a shrine my father built to celebrate himself. Hence the reflective surfaces. You heard my half brothers call it a morgue. He was a ghost throughout my childhood. Why not haunt my adulthood as well?"

"You're nothing like your father," Margot told him fiercely, and she didn't need the scientific method to achieve that conclusion. She knew.

"I never thought so. But then, Professor, the strangest things happen in sex hotels at the top of the world. A man who thinks he knows himself well might come to find that, unbeknownst to him, he has never been anything but a copy of the one man he hates above all others."

That shocked her, but she rallied. "I don't know what you're talking about. Nothing that happened last night makes you a man like that."

"It's all about intimacy, is it not?" Thor asked, a strange tension in his voice. She could feel it in the way he held himself. "Isn't that what we've been trying to fuck in and out of each other? And yet you can't live through a night like last night and not use it to take stock of all the other nights in your life, can you?"

"No," Margot said, and she didn't know if she was agreeing with him or denying what seemed to be coming next; what that knot of foreboding in her chest told her was surely coming next, no matter how she tried to hold on to him and the night they'd shared. With her fists.

"My father is famous for being a kind of sex god of his time. He has left the evidence littered about the planet in his wake. I have always been so certain that it was different when I did it. Because I am a different man. But perhaps that's the biggest lie of all and I am no different."

"Do you have a great many children out there that you refuse to acknowledge?"

"I have no children at all." Thor's mouth flattened. "As far as I know."

Margot told herself there was no reason she should feel so relieved to hear that. The man's sexual history was his business, not hers, and some people weren't parental…

But she had to fight to keep herself from grinning, because relieved was exactly what she felt.

"That's one difference," she said instead. "Another is that you're not cruel."

"You have no idea if that's true or not, Margot."
And it was as if he tried to prove it then, with that expression on his face that made her wonder if he wanted her to hurt. To wonder. To fight to keep her breath from going shallow. "You have no idea how I plan to extricate myself from this situation. Will I let you down easy? Will I tell you lies? Will I simply make myself unavailable again?"

Her heart was slamming at her, but Margot kept her gaze trained on him. And for the first time since she'd woken up this morning, she wished she wasn't naked.

"You could do something truly revolutionary and choose none of the above," she suggested as evenly as she could.

"I promised myself two things," Thor gritted out. "One, that I would never be my father. And yet I realize that I have made myself his twin. I sleep around, without thought for the feelings of others. I have fun, so I assume they must be having fun as well. But how would I know?"

"You would know. Of course you would know."

It was almost funny to imagine he might not, after the attention he'd paid to…everything last night.

But he ignored her. "And second, I vowed that I would never become like my mother. A slave to emotions that ruined lives. My stepfather's. Her own."

"Yours?" Margot dared to suggest.

He didn't like that. That was clear, though all he did was stare down at her, his icy gaze glittering.

"And in one night, one single night, I have betrayed myself completely."

Margot moved again then, without thinking it through. Because she was in a panic, bright and searing, and she didn't know what to do except climb over the back of the couch and slide to the ground. And then she stood there before him, her hands gripping the jacket of his suit as if it was some kind of harness. As if she could lead him somewhere. As if she could muscle him into doing what she wanted—

Even if she didn't know what it was she wanted.

"This is what family is," she told him fiercely. "No one feels that they fit. Everyone thinks that they're missing something, somehow. If you're lucky, there's enough love in the mix that it all balances out, or so I hear, because it wasn't as if my father was any easier."

Margot felt disloyal saying such a thing out loud. Worse, she felt weak. As if in acknowledging that her father had been something less than ideal, she was showing her true colors after all. She was showing how little she had always been worth, just as her father had always suspected.

And if she'd been alone, that might have wounded her. That might have given her pause, at the very least. But she was too focused on Thor to care.

"Even if you followed in your father's footsteps,

who cares?" she asked, because he'd handed her that napkin and freed her, somehow. And she wanted to do the same for him. "You're still not him. You'll never be him. You need to ask yourself why you think you have no choice in the matter."

She didn't miss the way her own words slammed into her, too. She didn't miss the fact that she'd never asked herself that question, either. What had she been trying to prove all this time? Why had she always allowed her father to make her feel, no matter what she did, that she didn't measure up?

And how could she tell Thor that he was the reason she was even capable of recognizing her own complicity in these things that had twisted her life around into something she wasn't sure she even wanted?

Margot didn't want to be a brain in a jar. She didn't want to hide in her words and her theories and her research.

She wanted to live her life, not study it.

With a quick breath for courage, she lifted herself up on her tiptoes and tilted her head back, because she knew exactly what she needed to do. She let go of his suit jacket and moved her hands up the hard-packed wall of his chest, every inch of which she'd tasted. Touched. And could likely re-create from memory, if necessary.

She looped her hands around his neck, letting her thumbs move over the splendor of his fine jaw.

"Margot."

Her name was a warning, but she didn't heed it. Instead, she lifted herself up even farther and went to press her lips to his.

But he stopped her. He reached up and took her upper arms in his hands, holding her away from him so she couldn't make contact.

"I want to kiss you," she said, and she knew, somehow, that it was more than a kiss.

That it was everything.

And more, she could see that he knew it, too. It was that gleaming light in his gaze, though his expression remained tortured.

It was everything, but he was keeping her from doing it.

"No," he said, as if the word was torn from him. "It's against the rules."

"I made the rules. I can break them, if I want."

"But I agreed to those rules. No kissing, Professor."

Margot didn't simply recognize the anguish she saw in his face then. She felt it, deep inside her. As if he was a part of her. As if he always would be, no matter what came next.

And she knew what was coming. She could see it. It was written all over him, and even though it was no more than they had agreed upon, it felt like the end of the world.

"Look out the window," he ordered her, though

his voice told her things she knew he wouldn't. "The snow has stopped."

She didn't have to look. She didn't want to look. If she'd been paying attention to something other than Thor, she would already have noticed the sunlight beaming into the room, as crisp and cold as he was.

"You were trapped in my hotel while the storm ran its course," Thor said, as if he was handing down a sentence. As if he was throwing them both into prison, forever. "And now it has."

"Thor…" The next word stuck in her throat, but she forced herself to keep going, because she didn't care about power differentials when her heart was breaking into pieces. "Please…"

"We had an agreement, Margot," Thor said, and just like that, the torment on his face disappeared. She watched it go, leaving nothing but ice behind. Until it was as if he had carved himself from the same volcanic rock that littered this island. It was as if he was nothing but sharp edges and the distant memory of ancient fires. As if the Thor she knew was gone. Or had never been at all. "And it's time for you to go."

CHAPTER NINE

EVERYTHING WAS FINE.

More than fine, as a matter of fact. Thor was not in the habit of having emotional responses to his sexual exploits, because there was no place for such absurdities in the face of a mere physical release, and he was determined that this should be no different.

Because it was no different, he told himself sternly.

The only thing that made his night with Margot unlike other nights he'd had was that she'd gotten a rare glimpse into the personal life Thor preferred to keep as private as possible—despite what everyone thought they knew about him, thanks to his successes and that damned will. It was an error he would have prevented if he'd thought it through that morning. And one he'd compounded by talking to her about things he never, ever discussed.

Never.

Thor had no idea why he'd done any of that—and he had no intention of ever repeating his mistakes.

There were some rules even he never broke.

The professor had left in a taxi Thor had ordered himself. And once she had gone, Thor took great pleasure in telling himself that he could breathe again. That the world made sense again. That the strange urges and feelings that he'd experienced during that storm were more about the storm than anything else. They weren't about Margot, because they couldn't have been.

Because that didn't make any sense.

That wasn't who Thor was.

Thor had spent the whole of his childhood watching the people in his life claim that love was the reason for all of their bad behavior. All of their weaknesses and vices. All of the cruelties they'd visited upon one another, whether by design or indifference.

Thor had no intention of falling into that trap himself. And he'd spent decades more or less immune to emotion, which was a terrific way to make certain he steered clear of it all.

This was no different, he assured himself. He was no different now than he'd ever been. It had been a long night, that was all.

He spent the next week congratulating himself on his wisdom in sending his purple-haired American on her way before he could confuse the issue further with more private thoughts he should never have shared with her.

And not only because he could see that sympathetic look on her face every time he closed his eyes.

Thor couldn't say he particularly cared for the revelations he'd had about how his behavior matched Daniel St. George's famously debauched approach to life in general and women in particular, but he could handle that. After all, there was an easy solution if a man no longer wished to be the kind of man-whore Daniel St. George had always been.

And Thor quickly discovered that abstaining from the pleasures of the flesh was far easier than he ever would have imagined.

He removed himself from the hotel a few days after Margot left, telling his staff that a change of scene was in order.

It was good to get back to his house in Reykjavík. To remind himself that his real life wasn't that brooding hotel, but one stuffed full of his art, his books and all the things he'd collected over the years to show he was not and never would be his father. He had no interest in spending his life in an antiseptic warehouse the way Daniel St. George had.

Thor spent his nights in his clubs in the city, doing his usual rounds to make sure they were all running as smoothly as he liked. He made note of every detail about each place, then sent his thoughts and suggestions to his managers ahead of the monthly managers' meetings he insisted upon.

It wasn't until he found himself standing out on

Laugavegur an hour or so before dawn one night, the bitter wind licking at him straight off the harbor, that he understood what he was doing.

He'd been so busy congratulating himself on taking a break from the hotel and his reputation that he'd somehow failed to notice that what he was really doing out here every night was looking for Margot.

And it was one thing to tell himself lies while he was tucked up in warmth and luxury. It was something else again when he was out in the thick, heavy dark of the approaching winter, just Thor and the night sky.

He found he didn't really try.

And the not trying felt a good deal like surrender.

Worse still, it appeared that his stubborn professor was full up on her research, because she was nowhere to be found. She wasn't in the bars or the clubs or any other of Reykjavík's hot spots—and this was Reykjavík. There were only so many places.

If she'd been out at night, conducting her interviews, he'd have run into her already.

Thor was standing out in the cold, pretending he was clearing his head after the loud live music he'd been listening to at the last bar.

He'd been pretending a lot of things lately, it seemed.

The truth was, Thor had been alone all his life, in one way or another. He had been alone in his parents' painful loop of unrequited love. He had been alone when he'd made his way in the world. He'd been alone when he'd built himself a tidy little empire and he'd certainly been alone throughout his adult life.

It had never occurred to him that there was another way.

And yet despite all of that, Thor had never been lonely.

Until now.

And he didn't know what the hell to do about it.

Margot locked herself in her bright and cozy little sublet, flatly refusing to entertain the dark emotions that traipsed around inside her. Instead, she threw herself into her work.

Because everything was different now. She could feel her shift in perspective like a kind of bone-deep tremor all throughout her body. It was a physical manifestation of what she'd done and said and felt that night at Thor's hotel and it made her hands ache. It made her legs feel weak even when she was lying down, scowling at her sloped ceiling, wishing herself asleep.

And she told herself she didn't mind if she carried the remnants of that night—and that napkin, and everything that had come after—with her forever. She knew she would. It was as if that night was a tattoo she wore on her skin, much brighter and more vibrant than the text she'd already put there.

Margot could choose to ignore the tattooed sensation and that trembling thing that lived in her now, every time she thought about Thor. Or she could try. But she was determined that her research reflect the change she'd lived through that night.

She flipped through all the notes she'd made on all those nights out in the city's bars and clubs. She listened to the voice recordings she'd made, imagining the faces of the people she'd met, and if she pretended that there wasn't one particular face that she saw above all, well…that was no one's business but hers.

She begged off from coffee dates and dinners her friendly colleagues invited her to and threw herself into her work with the kind of passion she remembered from way back in the last of her doctoral dissertation days.

That was the last time she had given herself permission to immerse herself in her research completely. She'd thrown herself into her dissertation and hunkered down with it until it was done at last. Until she couldn't quite tell the difference between the writing, the thinking and her. Until she wasn't sure where the words ended and she began, as a separate being.

Margot told herself it was a kind of freedom. Even a sort of bliss.

And she ignored the part of her that whispered that really what she was doing was hiding.

She restructured her arguments. She developed new theories.

"I still don't understand why you picked such a dramatically remote place to spend your sabbatical," her father told her with his usual condescension when she took a break from it all on Sunday evening to call her parents like the dutiful daughter she'd always been. "But I suppose Iceland is all the rage these days. As are treatises on sexuality, one supposes."

Margot burned with her usual shame and fury at that.

And normally she would have fallen all over herself to explain what she was doing. To try to make herself palatable to the one person alive who had never approved of a single thing she'd ever done—

But there was that tremor inside her. There was that ache in her fingers. There was the memory of the bluest eyes she'd ever seen and the approval in them that had made them seem lit on fire.

She wasn't the same person she'd been before she'd gone to Thor's hotel.

Maybe that was why she laughed instead of launching into the usual host of hurried explanations her father never paid much attention to anyway.

"I'm a tenured professor, not a teenager trying to be dramatic, Dad," she said, the same way she'd have laughed at a pompous student in one of her classes. "If the research I wanted to do could have been done in Des Moines, I would have gone there. I'm not in Iceland because it's trendy. I'm here because it's critical to my work."

Her father sputtered, and Margot braced herself for the flare of his temper—but instead, he handed the phone over to her mother quicker than he usually did.

Margot stood across the dark autumn arch of the planet, staring out her little window into the quickly coming night, and wondered why it had taken her so long to stand on her own two feet.

"What on earth did you say to your father?" her mother asked, muffling the receiver as if she was whispering. She likely was. Margot could see her as easily as if she was in the same house. Her mother was walking through the house from her father's study, back to the kitchen table, where she liked to spend her time. She read the paper there, listened to the radio and watched the kind of television that made Margot's father curl his lip in disgust.

Margot had always curled her lip in the exact same way at those shows, just to prove once again that she was nothing like her mother; that she was smart and intellectually curious and was worried about *weighty matters*, not the latest royal wedding or Hollywood scandal or silly movie-of-the-week.

"I think Dad forgets that he's not the only academic in the family," she told her mother, squeezing her eyes shut as if that could keep her from having to look at herself too closely.

Her mother let out a sound that could have been a sigh. Or a laugh.

"Your father forgets he's not the only academic alive," she replied after a moment. "It's part of his charm, really. But, Margot, you should know that no matter how he gets—and you know how he can get sometimes—he's so proud of all you've accomplished. We both are."

There was no reason Margot should have found herself blinking back tears at that. At another example of kindness from a person who she hadn't always treated well, so busy had she been trying to earn Ronald Cavendish's next distracted smile.

"I couldn't have done anything without you, Mom," she heard herself say, and it actually hurt as it came out.

Because it was true, and she hadn't understood that before. It was true, but Margot had been careening around all these years feeling superior to her own mother and the simple, steadfast love she'd always offered no matter the lip-curling or superiority complexes around her. Margot had always been so sure that kind of solidity and certainty was beneath her.

Maybe you've been emulating the wrong parent all this time, something inside her suggested. Harshly.

"I love you, too, honey," her mother was replying, sounding surprised—which also hurt. "Are you all right?"

If that wasn't an indictment, Margot didn't know what was.

"I'm perfectly fine," she told her mother.

And God, how she wanted that to be true, even if she wasn't sure she knew herself any longer. Maybe the truth was that she was finally figuring out the truth of who she should have been all this time.

No matter how much it hurt.

All in all, it was a full ten days later when she emerged, feeling shaky and strange, blinking her way into the bright, white light of a shockingly clear Reykjavík morning.

It was cold, the way it was always cold. She could feel the wind slice into her despite the fact she was wearing her heavy parka and good, warm boots. The air slapped at her face, making her eyes tear up and her skin feel chapped on contact.

Margot arranged her scarf to cover her mouth, then shoved her gloved hands into her pockets as she headed down her little street toward the busier, more central part of Reykjavík. She took deep breaths of the thin, frigid air and told herself it was time to accept the fact that there was no more avoiding the one subject she hadn't wanted to address at all.

Not directly.

If she pressed her lips together, she could still feel that napkin there, teaching her a thousand things about herself she hadn't wanted to know.

And what a funny thing it was that she could be brought so low by a simple bit of fabric and the man who'd offered it to her. She felt humbled, altered, and

she couldn't tell if that was a positive or negative—
not even all these days and a new interaction with her
parents later. Margot thought that really she should
have objected. Surely every feminist bone in her body
should have risen up in protest—

But that was the curious thing. She couldn't think
of anything more feminist than locating her own
voice, by any means possible. Did it matter how she'd
gotten to that point? Or was she trying to complicate
her own responses because she thought she should
have reached it on her own?

Was what had happened to her problematic—
or did she want it to be, so she could dismiss it?
Or shame herself into denying the experience had
changed her?

If another woman had told her that she'd had this
same experience, Margot would have found it hugely
concerning that a man had been the impetus for such
growth. She knew she would have.

But that was minimizing the experience. And
Margot didn't want to do that any longer. No more
airs of intellectual superiority to conceal all her worst
insecurities. And all the Bechdel tests and feminist
manifestos in the world couldn't change the fact that
it was the sex that had changed her.

And she was unaware of any way that a heterosexual woman could have life-altering sex without
a man.

Which meant, of course, that there was no way

not to put a man in the center of her own narrative. It was a notion that should have appalled her and yet…didn't.

Does it matter if we were both there at the center? she found herself asking as she walked down the cold streets. *Is sex only problematic when it's not intimate, or is it intimacy that's the real problem—because it knocks down all these barriers and leaves everyone both more and less than they were before?*

She could almost hear Thor's voice in her head as she turned that over and over inside her.

But then, the truth of the matter was that she could hear Thor's voice in her head all the time, and she wasn't sure she cared how problematic that was.

She hadn't believed in the kind of casual sex Icelanders engaged in before she'd experienced it herself. She still didn't. It was just that now Margot knew that it wasn't just hookup cultures or her generation's approach to dating that she found curious and flat. She had to look back at her entire sexual history and ask herself why she'd never understood that all the sex she'd ever had before Thor had…not been good.

Of course, she knew the answer.

She'd thought that the idea that sex could be fireworks and earthquakes, natural disasters and the northern lights all in one, were lies told in romance novels for the benefit of the feebleminded.

Margot had never imagined for a second that sex

like that was—or could be, or maybe even *should* be—real.

"You got exactly what you asked for," she told herself resolutely. "A bit more than that, maybe, but no less."

Her lack of imagination was her own damned fault.

She made herself walk past the coffee shop nearest to her flat where she knew a number of her university colleagues spent their time, because she didn't want to talk about any of this.

That concerned her, too, if she was honest. She felt as if Thor had freed her. He'd allowed her to find her voice in ways she never would have imagined possible, but it had left her loath to engage in the kind of conversations she'd used to find so entertaining. She didn't want to take a tiny point and dig at it, poke at it, tear it apart.

Her life before that night in Thor's hotel felt so small now, as if it had shrunk in the wash while she hadn't been paying attention.

Was it academics that had gotten narrow over the course of these tenured years? Or was it Margot's approach to scholarship?

When had she turned away from big questions and lost herself in the minutia instead?

It was that old saying that everyone liked to trot out in weary tones, usually after contentious meetings, that academic politics were so vicious because the stakes were so small.

And Margot couldn't seem to remember why she'd decided that what she needed from her life was a steady diet of small stakes and meaningless arguments. Especially not now she felt turned inside out and made anew.

She found herself a seat near the window in a quaint coffeehouse, packed with cozy couches and overstuffed bookcases, and shrugged out of her parka. It was still bright outside and the light streamed in, piercing and blue and maybe a little too intense, but Margot liked the feel of it on her face.

She'd spent so long in the dark—all those nights out on the Reykjavík streets, or holed up in her flat. Or that long, stormy night in Thor's hotel, for that matter.

Or her entire life and field of study.

Margot had almost forgotten the simple pleasure of sunlight. The warmth of it and the way it washed over her like a caress. The way the light poured in through windows and made it hard to see anything but all that bright, hot sun.

And maybe that was why it took her longer than it should have to notice the person who came to her side and stood there, backlit by the precious northern sunlight.

Margot shifted. Frowning by rote, she tried to make her eyes focus on the figure before her. She opened her mouth to comment on the numerous empty seats sprinkled throughout the coffeehouse at this hour on an indifferent Tuesday morning, but stopped herself.

Because her eyes might have been watering as she gazed into all that miraculous light, but her body knew exactly who she was looking at.

She felt herself shiver into instant awareness. She felt her pussy clench, then melt.

She knew.

Even before she lifted her hand to shade her eyes and really look at him, she knew.

"Hello, Professor," Thor said.

He sounded…not quite angry. Nothing quite so sharp. But he didn't sound his lazy, disengaged self, either.

Margot told herself there was no reason for her heart to flip around inside her chest at that notion.

"Thor," she said evenly, by way of greeting. "What are you doing here?"

He moved to the side so she could turn in her seat and look at him without having to stare directly into the sun. Not that it was any better. Thor was brighter by day. His eyes were too blue and the light picked up those impossible cheekbones and the mouthwatering line of his jaw. He wasn't dressed in that armored suit of his today, preferring boots and more casual trousers under the typical parka. He unzipped it against the heat in the coffeehouse, but he didn't sit down.

It took Margot a shockingly long moment to realize he was…whatever awkward looked like on a man like him.

Her stomach twisted into a knot, then flipped around deep inside her.

"Are you all right?" she asked.

"As a matter of fact, no." Thor stood there over her and she saw to her amazement that his big hands were in fists at his sides. She could hardly make sense of that, but there was no denying the way his eyes blazed when she lifted her gaze to his again. "I'm not all right, Margot. Where have you been?"

He did nothing to modify his volume or his tone, and Margot felt herself redden at the knowledge that the locals behind the counter might recognize him. Or even Margot, since she hadn't exactly been hiding her identity during all those late-night interviews.

She made herself smile. Politely. "I assume you mean that in a philosophical sense. Because I wasn't aware that I had to report my whereabouts to you. Or anyone else."

"You haven't been on Laugavegur, Margot. You haven't been accosting my customers. What am I supposed to make of that?"

"I don't know why you would care where I am." It cost her to keep her feelings off her face, but she thought she managed it. "You do remember that you told me to get out of your hotel, right?"

"We agreed that you would be there only as long

as the storm continued. The storm had ended, so it was time for you to get back to your life. It didn't mean you needed to drop off the face of the planet."

"I didn't drop off the face of the planet."

"It's been ten days."

He said that as if he was outraged that she might not know how long it had been, and that made the knot inside her catch fire.

"Thor." Margot indicated the seat across from her, nodding toward it, afraid that if she let herself she would…explode. Or something equally terrifying. "Would you like to sit down?"

"I would not like to sit down, Margot. What I would like is an explanation. Any explanation will do. Where have you been? Have you been hiding? Licking your wounds?"

That knotted thing pulsed, electric and so intense it bordered on pain.

"What wounds do you imagine I should be licking?" she asked, and she wasn't managing to keep herself calm and expressionless any longer. She could hear it in her voice and had no idea what was on her face. What felt revolutionary was that she didn't care. "You're the one who threw me out. Because I had the temerity to worry about your emotions, if I recall correctly. Not a mistake I plan to make again."

"That's the trouble," Thor threw at her. "I don't make mistakes and I don't have feelings."

"People don't generally track other people down in coffeehouses to shout at them about things they *don't* feel."

He looked as if she'd hit him. And she watched as he took one of those big fists and tapped it against the center of his chest.

"I don't want to feel this, Margot," he thundered at her. "I don't want to *feel* any of this. I don't want you inside me, so deep I don't remember my own damned name."

CHAPTER TEN

THOR FELT UNHINGED. BROKEN.

This was not how he operated. He did not skulk around the neighborhood he was pretty sure a past lover lived in, on the off chance that he might catch sight of her the way he had today. He did not make scenes. He certainly didn't lose his cool at past sexual partners—not least because he had never felt that deeply about any one of them.

But this was Margot. Everything was different with Margot.

He was different with Margot.

Thor had learned entirely too many things about himself over the past ten days. Chief among them that he'd been lying to himself for the bulk of his life without ever realizing it.

"I don't know what you're talking about," she was saying now, though the way she had her chin tilted into the air told him what a liar she was. "You must have told me a hundred times how Icelanders operate. All handshake, no feelings, because you're so *evolved*."

"While you, of course, hide away in this or that ivory tower to protect yourself with your research. Is that right?"

"As a matter of fact, that's exactly what I've been doing for the past ten days," she replied loftily. "Research."

Thor felt the edges of his vision go a little wobbly. "I beg your pardon. Exactly what kind of research?"

Margot smiled, sharp and edgy. "Why? Would it bother you if I spent every single one of the past ten nights conducting your favorite form of research with every Icelandic sex god I could find? Handshake after handshake?"

Thor wanted to deny it, of course. Because he was not a jealous man. He'd never understood those who were, when there were always other women, other lovers.

But there was only one Margot and he was already a mess, so why not admit it? It wasn't as if he was doing a great job of hiding it.

"Yes," he bit out. "It would bother the hell out of me."

And that sat there between them then, ugly and real.

Thor didn't know which one of them was more shocked. He, who had never been the slightest bit jealous of anyone or anything, thought he ought to have been appalled that such a sentiment existed inside him—much less had exited his mouth.

And he was quite certain that his progressive professor would have a similar take.

Margot cleared her throat, though her eyes looked darker than usual.

"I don't believe in possessiveness," she told him, though he thought her voice was awfully weak.

"Neither do I." He shrugged. "And yet here I am. Feeling more than a little fucking possessive, Margot. The question is—what are we going to do about it?"

She blinked, and he watched the way she sat up straighter, as if she was as affected as he was—but was hiding it better. And it was amazing how much he wanted that to be true.

"You mean, other than having a serious conversation about the deleterious effects of toxic masculinity?" She frowned at him. "Speaking of which, did you follow me here?"

"It's more accurate to say that I saw you on the street and decided to come say hello. Perfectly acceptable and social, no? Or is that not something you Americans understand?"

Her frown deepened. "Why were you on *this* street?"

"Here's the problem," Thor said then, because he didn't much like where this was going. "I should feel toxic, but I don't. I feel alive."

He expected her to descend into a full-on scowl,

but instead, she pulled in a breath as if he'd landed a blow. It was another thing Thor should have hated but found he didn't.

"You flipped a switch in me and I can't turn it off," he told her. "I haven't seen you in ten days, and yet you're the only thing I see. You know how I feel about ghosts, and yet you haunt me. Is this what you mean by toxic, Margot? Because I have the terrible feeling that it is something far more insidious."

She sat straighter in her chair and tilted that chin of hers higher, as if that would keep him from noticing that she'd gone a little pale. "Like what?"

Thor knew it was a taunt. A dare.

He should have hated it. He should have hated all of this.

But he couldn't quite get there, because this was Margot. This was who she was and who he was, too, when he was with her. He could go ten years without seeing her and he knew it would be exactly like this. She was bracing and she was beautiful and he was never going to get past this. Never.

The longer he looked at her, the less he wanted to.

"At first I told myself I didn't care because I have never cared before." He gazed down at her, as if he could change what happened that easily. "I came into the city and took my usual tours of my bars. My clubs. There's nothing new or special about it. I go back and forth between Reykjavík and the hotel all the time and I take my pleasure as it is presented to me. I like sex, as you might have comprehended."

"I don't believe in sexual jealousy," she told him loftily, but he could see the color high on her cheeks and the way her lips formed a flat line.

"I don't believe in it, either. But you don't have to believe in something to feel it, do you?" Margot scowled at him, and that eased the hard knot in his chest that had been getting harder, sharper, thicker by the day. "But this is what I'm trying to tell you. No one would do. No one interested me. It isn't that I haven't touched another woman since you, Margot. It is that I haven't had the slightest urge."

"I don't know how you want me to respond to that. You can't possibly expect me to take responsibility for your feelings. Nor, I hope, are you anticipating that I will congratulate you on a little spell of abstinence."

"You are all I see," he told her again, more intensely this time. "At first I told myself I was looking for a woman who interested me, whoever she might have been. One night passed. Two nights. Three. And soon I was forced to admit the truth. I don't want another woman. I want you. Only you. Tell me what I'm supposed to do with that."

She made a noise that could have been anger. All of this was new to Thor. He couldn't recall having this kind of overwrought conversation with anyone. Ever. It veered too close to the sort of maudlin carrying-on that he associated with his mother, when she'd had far too much to drink.

But it was early in the morning. It was bright and clear. He was perfectly sober.

And Margot might have been looking at him as if she didn't comprehend a single word he was saying— but he could see her hands there in her lap, balled up into fists so tight that he was certain her fingernails would leave marks on her palms when she unfurled them.

And he knew, somehow.

Just as he'd known during that long, epic night they'd spent together. He might not know what she wanted. But he seemed to have no trouble at all in- tuiting what she needed.

And maybe it didn't matter that it took him a little longer to figure it out for himself.

"Let me tell you how I've spent the last ten days," he told her. He didn't care that he was a recogniz- able figure in the city, or that at least two patrons in this coffeehouse were likely filming him as he stood here, making a fool of himself. She had put that napkin in her mouth. The least he could do was use his voice, too. "First I looked for someone to help me forget you. But that didn't work, because I do not think it will be possible to forget you. When I finally admitted that to myself, I began to look for you. Yet you were nowhere."

"Not that it's any of your business," she said, her

voice tight and her body stiff and unfriendly, "but I locked myself in my flat with my research. My research notes, that is. Today is the first day I've come up for air."

He recognized that sheen of moisture in her eyes. It told him she knew exactly the gifts she'd given him. And how could he help but try to be worthy of them?

"You think I don't understand this," he said quietly. "But I do. It's too complicated. It's too overwhelming. It's not at all what you wanted. Don't you think it took me by surprise, too?"

"I'm sure you have nights like that all the time."

"You know I don't. And neither do you."

"It was a really great handshake," she said, and there was something stark on her face. It made Thor feel raw inside. Scraped out. Hollow. "And I appreciate you coming to tell me that you had the same experience. But it was only a handshake, Thor. That was the agreement."

"I want a new agreement."

The winter sun was streaming in through the coffeehouse's front window, making Margot look ethereal. Otherworldly. As if she was one of Iceland's magical creatures, brought to life there before him. Her lavender hair seemed to glow like some kind of halo around her and that mouth of hers was enough to send him over the edge.

She looked wild. Hurt.

His.

And that was the part he concentrated on when she shook her head, shoved back from her table and surged to her feet.

"No," she said fiercely, her voice low and shaking at the edges. "I can't. One taste was more than enough. I don't want any more. I can't take any more."

Thor was close enough to see the very moment her frown trembled into something else, her face falling as the emotion in her eyes tipped over at the edges.

And he could tell that it horrified her. He saw it on her face in that split second before she pushed past him and threw herself out into the cold.

But Thor had suffered through ten long days and even longer nights. He'd had no choice but to accept who he was.

It was easy to beat himself up for his excesses and call himself Daniel St. George the Second.

But the truth was, Thor was like his father. His real father, Ragnar. The man who had fallen in love once and had never been dissuaded from that path, no matter what. The man who had loved Thor's mother and Thor himself with a quiet steadfastness that Thor could still feel inside him, as if that love was in his bones. As if it *was* his bones.

A man only truly falls in love once, Ragnar had told him once. *But if he is lucky, once is all he needs.*

Thor had always thought that was just another example of the kind of pure foolishness he wanted nothing to do with.

Then he'd met Margot and everything had changed.

He hadn't fallen apart that night in his hotel, though in many ways that was what it felt like.

He was terribly afraid he'd fallen a whole lot further.

And it was entirely possible that he was more like his lost, lamented father than he wanted to admit. To Margot, their one night might have been exactly that—one night.

But there was only one way to find out, and he didn't much care if it offended her sensibilities.

Thor threw open the coffeehouse door and went after her.

Margot told herself she was blinded by the winter sunshine, but that was a lie.

She was crying and she hated it, so she ran.

She ran away from the coffeehouse. From Thor.

From all the intense emotions that swirled around between them until she thought she might choke on them—and then what would become of her?

She ran until her lungs hurt, until she ran out of pavement, and found herself there at the edge of the harbor. There were big, broken-up chunks of ice floating out in the water and snow-covered mountains in the distance and every inhalation made her nose hurt. When she turned back around, she knew she would be charmed all over again by the brightly painted buildings clustered together that made up

Europe's most northern city. It was easy to fall in love with Reykjavík.

But when she turned around, the only thing she saw behind her was Thor.

"Why are you following me?" she demanded, but she hardly recognized her own voice. Or the dark things that flooded her, as if she was a different person. The kind of person whose heart leaped at the sight of him. The kind of woman who wanted things she'd been taught to think were bad and wrong and beneath her.

Such as a beautiful man she couldn't stop thinking of chasing her through a city because he'd learned her. He knew her. And he'd taught her something, too—that her mouth would always argue when her body wanted nothing more than to surrender.

That mouth of his curved as he gazed down at her, as if the cold didn't bother him. "Tell me to leave you alone, Professor. Tell me that is what you want, and you will never see me again. I promise."

And of course that was what she wanted. It was what she needed, because she couldn't concentrate when he was near her and she shouldn't want the things he made her yearn for. She turned into someone she hardly knew when he was near. And anyway, she had work to do and papers to write and a life to get back to that didn't involve tall, dangerous Vikings who looked at her as if she was the only light left in this cold place.

Or the only light in him.

And as she stood there on the edge of the world, trapped between the frigid harbor and the thousand summers she saw in his blue eyes that seemed to gleam even brighter out here in all the remarkable daylight, she couldn't seem to say a word.

"You've ruined me," she whispered after much too long had passed and she thought the things she really, truly wanted were written all over her anyway.

Thor laughed at that. As if it—she—delighted him. "I believe I will take that as praise."

"Philosophically, I'm deeply opposed to these old, tired heterosexual norms," she seethed at him, because her heart kept pounding at her, but she couldn't seem to stop her mouth. She had managed it only once in as long as she could remember—but she didn't want to think about that now. Not here. "I'm outraged that any of this is happening. I don't want to feel these things, either, Thor. I spent my life deeply certain that I could never, ever feel these things."

"Funny. You tasted straight to me."

Margot knew she was lost because that sang in her, then settled like wine and heat in her pussy, which had never been confused about this man. And still wasn't.

But she wasn't ready to surrender. Not again.

"I never reacted to any man like all the songs said I should—or the movies, the books, the fairy tales. I always assumed that really, deep down, I wasn't like all the girls who felt those things. I thought I was different."

Because she'd wanted, desperately, to be different, she could admit to herself here. Now. She'd wanted to distinguish herself from the other girls she knew, and one way to do that was to create a lot of theoretical sexualities. She'd tried any number of them on for size, at least in her head. Because she'd wanted to be smarter, yes, and she'd wanted to impress her father. But more than anything, she hadn't wanted to feel ordinary.

And the fact that she'd only ever been attracted to men had seemed like a minor detail, nothing more.

Thor reached over and took a strand of her hair between his fingers, then seemed to concentrate on wrapping it around and around into a kind of thick purple ring.

Even the hair, Margot could admit to herself here, had been another way to prove she wasn't like the herd.

She didn't understand how this man could make her feel profoundly ordinary in a way that made something in her glow like molten heat, simply because he was a man and she was a woman—and unlike anyone else in the world, ever, just because he was looking at her as if she was made of pure magic.

"What does *different* mean?" he asked almost idly. "It sounds like an unnecessary label. Why don't you permit yourself to feel whatever it is that you feel without worrying what word to use to describe it."

"You kicked me out," she flared at him.

"You can tell me that I hurt your feelings, Margot," he said quietly, his blue gaze touching hers as if he knew. As if she was still naked when she was with him, no matter what she was wearing. "You don't have to pretend you don't care."

Margot swallowed. Hard.

"I care," she whispered.

She felt as if she'd screamed out her feelings to the whole of Iceland. As if she'd revealed so much of herself that she might as well really have been standing there in the cold, as stripped down as she'd been in his hotel. And she thought that if he smirked at her, if he made some kind of joke, if he did anything at all, she might not survive it.

But Thor only smiled.

"I know. And I'm glad."

"Because it gives you the upper hand?" she asked sharply, because she was afraid of that, too. She was afraid of everything.

"Pay attention, please, Professor." He tugged on her hair, a sharp little bite that echoed everywhere. "I don't want the upper hand, necessarily. What I want is you."

Something wild and sharp shot through her. Her first thought was that it was some kind of virus, taking out her knees right here in public.

It took one long breath, then another, to realize that it was joy.

She wasn't sure she'd ever felt anything like it before.

But she also wasn't sure she dared let herself believe it. "You had me."

"It turns out that one night was too brief a time. I am thinking of something longer. To allow for far more…research opportunities. Perhaps a year?"

"You can't possibly mean that. You hardly know me."

"I know you," Thor corrected her. And there was something about the way he said it. About that pure confidence in his gaze and stamped all over his face, as if he was telling her one of the Icelandic sagas. "I may not know every detail. There are a thousand stories we have yet to tell each other, but we will, in time. Still, I know you. And what's more, Margot, you know that I do. You were there. You know exactly how intimate we were over the course of one long night. You know what it meant."

She heard a ragged sound and only dimly understood it was her. Her breath. Her heart. She couldn't tell the difference.

"I don't know what you mean."

"I mean that I want you. In my bed. In my life. All of the above."

"I don't believe in things like this," she told him fiercely, while her heart clattered in her chest. "I don't believe it's possible. One night is just one night, and it doesn't magically turn into…" But she couldn't say that word, no matter how blue Thor's gaze was. "A relationship is a deep friendship over the course of time. It's an egalitarian partnership. It's supporting each other, learning how to be disappointed in each other. It's choosing to stay with another person despite all the weight and baggage of reality and experience."

"That sounds like a prison sentence." Thor's voice was dry, though his blue eyes danced with laughter. "Here in Iceland there was a survey. Most of us said, when asked, that we refused to deny the existence of trolls, elves and other magical creatures."

"I've heard that statistic. I think it was on the flight I took over here, in fact. But I don't think—"

"I was raised on the sagas, Margot," Thor said. He shrugged, though his gaze never left hers. "Trolls and elves make as much sense to me as the aurora in winter, the white nights of summer and, yes, a single night that feels like forever. Why not? Who are you to determine how much time is enough to know you need another person in your life?"

"Because it's supposed to be hard!" she threw at him.

But this was Thor. He only smiled back at her as if these were love songs she was singing, not arguments she was trying to make. "Why?"

Margot felt as desperate as she had when she'd decided to strip off her clothes in his bedchamber because he'd dared her to enact her consent. As desperate as she had when he'd presented her with that napkin.

"Because I know who I am," she told him, the words spilling out of her mouth before she could think better of them and hold them back. "I'm a disappointment. Don't you understand? I'm glad you threw me out of your hotel. I'm glad it was only one night, and that you didn't let me kiss you. It's for the best. I think what we should do is agree to let this just be a memory. It's better that way. You don't want any part of who I really am, I promise you that."

He looked singularly unmoved by her confession. "Why not?"

"Every boyfriend I've ever had left me because I'm too independent."

"I'm an Icelander. We are the most feminist country in the world. Ask anyone. I was raised to prize independence in a woman, and I do."

"That's what they all said, but that's not what they meant." She shook her head, scowling at him. "I'm selfish. I lose myself in my work and I don't come out, sometimes for ten days at a time. I disappear, sometimes when I'm standing right in front of another person. I live in my head."

"Not always," Thor drawled, and she hated the fire that licked over her because it wasn't his mouth. His clever hands.

"I'm serious. I can't possibly give you what you want. I can't give—"

"Professor. All of this carrying-on because you don't want to admit that you are besotted with me is unseemly." He shook his head sadly, though his eyes danced. "I don't require you to make any declarations. Not now. Someday soon, I'll tie you up, shall I? And see what sort of truths I can coax out of you with my mouth. My hands. My cock, which we both know full well you love unreservedly."

Margot felt too hot. Too weak. And she wanted too much.

For the first time in her life, she wanted everything. The kind of relationship she'd described, steeped in reality. And the fantastical relationship she'd decided a long time ago wasn't possible. Sex like dying and being reborn, over and over and over again. Orgasms and laughter and a man who took her breath away without even trying.

She wanted it all.

"I'm not at all comfortable with those sorts of power dynamics," she lied.

Thor laughed. "I don't believe that any good comes out of deciding what you are and are not interested in. Or standing here, at a clinical distance, coming up with rules to live by. What's the point? You could make a list of things you're opposed to in bed, and maybe you mean it, but it's all abstract. When there is only me and you, alone, who can say what might happen? Why must we decide now?"

"I hope that's a roundabout way of saying that if you get to tie me up, I can tie you up, too."

"I don't know how you have failed to recognize

that I do not have the—what do you call them—
hang-ups that you seem to have." Thor's grin was
pure wickedness, and Margot couldn't pretend she
didn't want to bathe in it. In him. "You can do whatever you like to me. In fact, I encourage it. But I need
more time. More than one night, one storm."

And the world seemed to spin all around her,
too bright and too cold, so fast and so wild that she
should have felt dizzy.

But Thor's gaze was steady. And so blue. And
somehow, he helped her feel solid. Sturdy.

And there were so many things she wanted to
say. Arguments she wanted to make and justifica-
tions she wanted to throw out between them, to get
a little breathing room. To gain a little perspective.

Because you'd rather be in control than be happy,
a voice inside told her.

And sounded entirely too much like her mother.

Thor's fingers were still in her hair. And he wanted
her.

Not just for another night. A year, he'd said.

And that was the only word that made any sense
at all.

She didn't believe that anyone could fall for someone that fast, except she had. *They* had. She couldn't
believe that intimacy was possible without time and
trust, but she knew that night had proved otherwise.

She knew too many things that couldn't be true,
but somehow were.

Maybe she was only trying to argue because she didn't know what else to do.

Margot remembered the stark, empty penthouse in the hotel. How panicked she'd been when she put that napkin in her own mouth. And how quiet she'd gotten inside once she'd surrendered to it.

She did the same thing now.

She breathed out, long and slow. She surrendered. She moved closer to Thor, tipped her head up and let her gaze meet his.

And this time, when she pushed herself up onto her toes, then pressed her lips to his, he didn't stop her.

And that was how she kissed Thor for the very first time.

First it was a press of lips, as sweet as it was soft.

"Professor, I am not a fairy-tale princess in a drugged slumber," Thor said against her mouth. "I want more."

"Then take it," she invited him, because she understood now, with his taste in her mouth.

Surrender wasn't weak at all. Surrender was strong. It required the strength and the suppleness to bend without breaking. It required grace.

It required a heart full of trust. It required faith.

Thor angled his head and everything changed all over again.

Fire. Heat. And that greedy yearning that had been eating away at Margot since the moment she'd looked up to find him at her table in the middle of that storm.

He took and he took, as if he'd waited whole lifetimes to taste her like this. She found her hands in his hair and felt his around her face.

Still she kissed him, as if her life depended on it, too.

As if all this time, and no matter her brain or her job or her thoughts to the contrary, she had been something less than whole.

Wandering around, acting as if she knew things, when all the while her life had been leading her here. Right here.

To a perfect kiss from the perfect man, draped in all this bright, impossible sunlight in the middle of a cold fall, here at the top of the world.

"I am no professor," Thor said against her mouth, so she could feel the way his curved into a smile. "But this feels a whole lot like forever."

She couldn't help herself from smiling back, wide and filled with that joy so sharp it almost hurt.

"Come," she said, a thousand forevers in her voice, pumping like heat in her veins, and settling hot and needy between her legs. She took his hands in hers and tugged him along with her as she started for her flat. "I'll show you."

And that was exactly what she did.

CHAPTER ELEVEN

A YEAR LATER, Margot sat once again in the dimly lit bar of Hotel Viking, tucked away in a booth that offered her a view of nothing save the sea.

That surly, northern sea that crashed against the volcanic rocks far below, over and over again, with a kind of focused ruthlessness that made her shiver.

Much like the man she'd come here to see.

It had been the best year of her life.

Margot had spent the rest of her sabbatical in Reykjavík, but everything had changed. Thor took her to the house he kept in the city itself, where she learned more about him from the things he'd collected—and the distinction he drew between his true home and that hotel penthouse—than she'd known about some of the men she'd had entire relationships with.

He had encouraged her to give up her flat. She had refused, obviously, then had spent the whole of the next semester regretting that choice. Because she had been back in Iowa then, teaching and resuming her real life, and it had felt as if she'd left everything that mattered to her across the planet.

It didn't matter how many times Thor came to visit her. It didn't matter how many cold Iowa winter mornings she woke to find her favorite Viking there in her bed in the little house she kept within walking distance of the university.

Because there were always the mornings that followed. The mornings when she woke up and missed him so much it felt as if she might never be whole again.

Margot spent a lot of time interrogating her feelings, which she could only call operatic in the extreme, but that was the craziest part.

All the interrogation in the world didn't change them.

"I have a confession to make," she'd told Thor on one of their video calls, which she found torturous. She could see him. She could lose herself in the blue of his gaze, the sharp blades of his cheekbones. She could let his voice wrap around her. But she couldn't touch him, and it stunned her how much that hurt.

"That sounds ominous," he'd murmured in reply, lounging before her in all his indolence. "Not least because neither one of us is Catholic."

"There's a visiting professorship at the University of Iceland." She threw it out there, as if she'd been shooting a gun. "I applied. And, unless you have an objection, I start in the fall."

"What objection do you imagine I would have?" Thor had shaken his head, those eyes of his gleaming bright. "I will, of course, miss these mad flights into the American heartland at least once a month. I will miss the distance between us, which both of us have enjoyed so much. Do these count as objections?"

"You might feel differently when—"

"Professor." His smile had lodged inside her, where it always turned over and became heat. "Come."

Margot hadn't waited for the fall. As soon as classes had wrapped up in the spring, she'd packed up her house, put most of her belongings into storage and gone back to Reykjavík.

She had moved into the same flat and had pretended to not quite hear Thor's disgust on that subject.

But it hadn't mattered.

Because they had spent the whole of the previous spring semester building exactly the kind of friendship she'd always imagined a relationship should contain. They'd spent hours and hours talking through screens. They'd cooked meals together, separated only by the screens of laptop computers. They'd told stories, had drifted off to sleep with their electronic connections still open between them and had learned all the day-to-day truths about each other's lives. The routines. The drudgeries and small triumphs. The irritations and sweetnesses in turn.

Had that been all they did, Margot still would

have counted it as the most successful and exciting relationship she'd ever had.

But, of course, there had also been the visits.

She had flown back to Iceland for her spring break, where Thor had been as good as his word. He had asked her to trust him, and she had.

And he had stripped her down, blindfolded her and introduced her to his dungeon.

Where he had tied her up, made her cry and cry out, until she hardly knew who she was.

Then he had taken the blindfold off to reveal that there was no one else in the Hotel Viking dungeon but the two of them.

"I thought the point of a place like this was committing to a performance," Margot had said when Thor had finally untied her. "I expected a crowd."

"I would never toss you before a crowd without asking you first," he had murmured. "If public sex intrigues, only say the word."

But the truth was, Margot didn't particularly want to share him.

Something she thought she'd proved when she had taken her time returning the favor, tying Thor up so she could have her way with him.

Until they were both shaking.

It had been hard to sit still on her flight home, reliving all those delicious, deliriously intense moments with him.

Just as it had been hard to go back to that real life
of hers that didn't seem to fit her anymore.

Because she wanted him.

If anything, time made it worse.

They spent the long, bright summer together again
in Reykjavík. In her flat. At his house. And then back
at the hotel, when Thor felt they needed that little
touch of opera.

Summer days rolled into those Iceland summer
nights, bright as day, with a sun that never quite
dipped below the horizon.

"Why doesn't this drive you crazy?" she had
asked one night.

They had enjoyed a remarkably European evening. They had gone to a classical concert at Harpa,
the iconic concert hall on the water in Reykjavík.
Then they'd indulged in a late dinner. They had
walked back to Thor's house at midnight that looked
like noon.

Then they had enjoyed each other for dessert.

And had gone back for seconds.

"Do you mean the white nights?" Thor had asked,
from where he stood beside her at the windows she'd
opened because she still couldn't get used to all the
light at two in the morning. "Or the fact you still refuse to consider living with me?"

"We've gone over this. Virginia Woolf—"

"I own a hotel, Professor. If you must have a room
of your own, you have a variety to choose from."

"I want to enjoy the summer," she had whispered, fiercely.

Because, she realized now as she stared out at the surging sea, holding a glass of wine to her lips without tasting it, she hadn't expected it to last.

She had told herself, over and over again during the spring semester and again this long summer, not to get too comfortable. Not to put too many expectations on him. Or herself.

Summer had ended. The night had returned and then started to take over.

Margot had started her new job, and that had taken a lot of her concentration at first. She had thrown herself into the work, and a part of her had known full well that this was usually the breaking point. Her previous relationships had always shattered over the amount of time she dedicated to academics.

So it had been something of a surprise that Thor had no problem at all with how much she worked.

"I can't see you again until next week," she had said once, scowling at him in the street outside her flat. "I can't ask you up, as I'm getting up too early in the morning—"

"Professor. You wound me. Perhaps you have forgotten that I'm a vastly wealthy and terribly busy man."

"I haven't forgotten that. Why are you mentioning it?"

"It is not an act of surrender to share your schedule," he said drily. "On the contrary. It is how two busy people make sure they see each other when they can."

Margot had never known anyone like him.

When he told her that he would never resent her career, the truth was, she hadn't believed him. In her experience, that was the thing that men said—until the moment they wanted something and couldn't have it because she was tied up with work.

But Thor had a busy schedule of his own. Sometimes he needed to stay at the hotel rather than in town, even if that meant he couldn't see Margot. Sometimes he traveled out of Reykjavík. He always invited her along, but it never seemed to irritate him if she had to decline the invitation.

As the days passed, Margot began to believe.

That everything Thor had told her—that first, glorious night, and all the days thereafter—was true.

"You look entirely too pleased with yourself," came his voice then, washing over Margot the way the tide caressed the rocks below.

She took her time looking up at him. Up, then up some more.

He was beautiful. He was her Viking, summer blue eyes and the heat in them that she knew, now, was all for her.

"I was thinking about independence," she said.

This was a man who wanted her, always. She knew it when his gaze lit with that laughter she craved. She knew it when he lowered that big body of his to sit next to her on the banquette.

He wanted her body. He made that clear, nightly.

But he also adored her mind.

And somehow, she realized a little bit breathlessly, over the course of this past year he had fused the two together.

Somehow, he had made her whole.

Though it was more than that. It was the two of them, together.

Together, they could do anything. Long distance. Operatic sex. Quiet laughter. The inevitable fights. The intense makeup sessions.

Anything.

"Are you planning to assert your independence?" Thor asked. "While naked, a man can only hope."

"I always thought that I had to choose," she said. She had meant to keep her voice even. Steady. But then the words came out of her mouth and there was nothing steady about them.

The steady thing was the way Thor looked at her. It was the way he waited to see what she might say next. It was his body pressed against hers, ready to keep her safe no matter what came next.

"I never believed that I could have everything," she told him. "You're supposed to be impossible."

And he gazed at her for what felt like another forever or two. Then, slowly, he smiled.

"I love you, too, Margot."

That took her breath away.

But then she scowled at him, all the more ferociously when his smile widened.

"You don't even have to think about it. You're just going to throw that out there."

"Professor." Thor shifted in his seat, and Margot thought he was going to face her, that was all. But instead he lifted her up off the seat, holding her with that ease that never failed to make her wet and hot and needy, before settling her down astride his lap. "Catch up. I was in love with you before morning. But you needed a year to think about it."

"Nobody falls in love overnight."

But her voice was too thready. Too insubstantial.

"I did." His blue eyes blazed. "We did."

She could feel his cock between them, proud and ready, she couldn't seem to keep herself from moving her hips so she dragged her aching pussy over that hard ridge. She knew no one could see them, not with the high back of the banquette seat to block them from prying eyes—but tonight, she wasn't sure she cared.

"Thor..." she whispered.

As if his name really was a prayer.

Thor settled his big hands on either side of her face, smoothing back the hair she still kept lavender, not because she thought it made her different but because he loved it.

"I love you," he told her, and his voice was as hard

and sure as the volcanic rock the hotel sat upon. "I want you in every way a man can want a woman. I want to marry you. I want a family with you. I want to take care of you and let you take care of me in turn. I want to possess you and protect you, but only if you promise you will do the same for me."

"I promise," Margot whispered. And she leaned forward, tipping her face to his. "I love you, Thor."

"I know you do, Professor," he said, there against her mouth. "You had to think your way into it, that is all. Have I passed all your tests now?"

Margot wanted to argue. She opened her mouth to tell him that there were no tests, there was only time—

But that would have been a lie.

"I might have loved you that first night," she told him, solemnly, as if they were exchanging vows. Perhaps they were. "But I love you even more for waiting all this time."

"Professor. Margot." Thor's voice was soft, but that look in his eyes made a loud, chaotic kind of joy tumble through her. "I will always wait for you."

She kissed him then, because she was his.

And more wonderful still, he was hers. Truly hers.

"I love you," she told him again. Because now that she had said it, now that she had finally said it, she wanted to say nothing else. "I love you."

And for a long while, there was nothing but that love. His mouth on hers. His hands holding her jaw

where he wanted it, while she tortured them both
with the slick, soft roll of her hips.

Until Margot was tempted to imagine that they'd
made their own storm.

That they would always be the storm, this storm,
perfect and wild and beautiful, and entirely theirs.

Thor stood in a rush, taking Margot with him and
setting her on her feet.

"I have plans for you," he told her, and she could
feel the dark promise in his smile wind through her.
"All you have to do is make a single, simple choice."

Margot smiled, because none of the choices Thor
offered her were simple.

They were always far more complicated than they
seemed.

But they always made her scream.

She held his gaze, realizing that she'd trusted him
like this from the start. Some part of her had recognized him the moment she'd seen him. Some part of
her had known.

Margot didn't believe in love at first sight.

But she'd spent enough time in Iceland now to
know that only a fool bet against magic in a place
like this.

"Up or down?" Thor asked her, lazily.

Heat licked over her skin. Her nipples stood, aching. And her pussy was already wet with greed.

Up meant the penthouse, in all its stark beauty,

where every touch felt sacred and usually ended in prayers to some or other god.

Down meant the Hotel Viking dungeon, where there was nothing to do but turn the sacred inside out.

"You choose," she told him, because she didn't need rules and boundaries to love him. Not anymore.

This was love. And love was trust.

This was who they were.

It was who they'd been that first night, little as Margot had wanted to admit it. It was who they would always be, together.

Thor's smile sent flames racing all over her, and he was still smiling when he bent his head.

And when she surged to her toes to kiss him this time, Margot knew why he had always tasted like this.

At last, she knew.

Because Thor tasted like forever.

And forever started now.

* * * * *

COMING SOON!

We really hope you enjoyed reading this book. If you're looking for more romance, be sure to head to the shops when new books are available on

Thursday
1st November

MILLS & BOON

LET'S TALK
Romance

For exclusive extracts, competitions
and special offers, find us online:

f facebook.com/millsandboon

🅞 @millsandboonuk

🐦 @millsandboon

Or get in touch on 0844 844 1351*

For all the latest titles coming soon, visit
millsandboon.co.uk/nextmonth